BRER RABBIT
PLAYS A TRICK

and other stories

Illustrated by
Edgar Hodges

World International Publishing Limited
Manchester

Published in Great Britain by World International
Publishing Limited,
An Egmont Company, Egmont House, PO Box 111,
Great Ducie Street,
Manchester M60 3BL.
Printed in Italy.

British Library Cataloguing in Publication Data
Blyton, Enid 1897–1968
Brer Rabbit plays a trick and other stories.
I. Title
823.912 [J]

ISBN 0–7498–0298–7

Cover illustration by Robin Lawrie

Contents

Enid Blyton

Enid Blyton was born in London in 1897. Her childhood was spent in Beckenham, Kent, and as a child she began to write poems, stories and plays. She trained to be a teacher but she devoted her whole life to being a children's author. Her first book was a collection of poems for children, published in 1922. In 1926 she began to write a weekly magazine for children called *Sunny Stories*, and it was here that many of her most popular stories and characters first appeared. The magazine was immensely popular and in 1953 it became *The Enid Blyton Magazine*.

She wrote more than 600 books for children and many of her most popular series are still published all over the world. Her books have been translated into over 30 languages. Enid Blyton died in 1968.

Brer Rabbit plays a trick

Once Brer Rabbit had a fine crop of pickling onions, and he stood and looked at them, wondering what to do with so many.

"I've pickled all I want for myself," he said to Brer Terrapin, "and you don't like onions. What am I to do with so many, Brer Terrapin?"

"Pickle them in big jars and sell them to Mr Benjamin Ram!" said Brer Terrapin. "He's fond of onions, he is. He'll pay you a good price for them, Brer Rabbit. You get some good big jars and pickle the biggest onions you've got!"

So Brer Rabbit got some enormous stone jars and filled them full of onions in vinegar – my, how good they smelt!

Brer Terrapin sniffed them and wished he liked them. "Now, you ask old Benjamin Ram to dinner," he said, "and let him taste those. If he doesn't buy the whole lot from you I'll eat my shell!"

Mr Benjamin Ram came to dinner, and brought his violin. *Plink, plonk, plonk!* it went, as Brer Rabbit set out the dinner. Then Mr Benjamin Ram stopped his playing and sniffed.

"What's that nice smell?" he said.

"My pickled onions," said Brer Rabbit. "I know you're fond of them, Benjamin Ram."

He certainly was! He ate twenty-one, and Brer Rabbit marvelled at him.

Then he pushed back his chair, wiped his long beard, and said, "Best I've ever tasted. Ask me to dinner again, Brer Rabbit."

"I've got plenty of pickled onions to sell," said Brer Rabbit. "Cheap, too."

"Then I'll buy them – the whole lot!" said Mr Benjamin Ram. "Here you are

– here's my purse. Empty it, and let me have all the jars of onions you've got."

There was a lot of money in Mr Ram's purse. Brer Rabbit emptied it into his own pocket, very pleased. Then he got down the big jars of pickled onions from the shelves in his cupboard.

"There you are," he said. "Eight fine jars – enough to last you a month, Benjamin Ram. Shall I put them into a sack for you?"

"No," said Benjamin Ram. "I'm going to visit my old aunt, Bessie Ram – and she's fonder of pickled onions than I am. She would eat the lot. You deliver them for me, Brer Rabbit. I've paid you enough money for that, too."

He said goodnight and went, playing his violin all the way through the wood. Brer Rabbit could hear it – *plink, plonk, plunk, plink, plonk, plunk!*

He looked at the eight big jars. How was he going to carry all those? They were very, very heavy.

"If I carry them all at once, I'll never get there," thought Brer Rabbit. "And if I take them one at a time it would mean eight long journeys there and back."

He sat and thought hard. He saw someone passing his front gate – it was old Brer Bear carrying a sack of potatoes back home. It was a big heavy sack, but Brer Bear didn't mind. He was stronger than anyone else in the wood.

Brer Rabbit stared after him, and an idea began to bubble in his mind. Yes, *he* knew how to get those jars of pickled onions to Mr Benjamin Ram! Aha – it would be easy.

Brer Bear lived quite near Mr Benjamin Ram. Why shouldn't *he* carry a large sack full of jars of pickled onions all the way to Benjamin's house – and save Brer Rabbit's poor old back?

But it wouldn't be any good *asking* Brer Bear to do that. He was a surly fellow, and he wasn't at all fond of wily Brer Rabbit. No, Brer Rabbit would have to make him carry them by some clever little trick!

But what trick could it be?

Brer Rabbit sat with his head in his hands and his ears down, thinking hard again. And then his furry ears rose up straight and Brer Rabbit laughed out loud. "Of course! *I* know how to make Brer Bear carry my jars of pickled onions for me! Look out now, Brer Bear, you're going to have a heavy load soon!"

Well, what did Brer Rabbit do but take off all the labels on his jars that said PICKLED ONIONS and put another set on instead. On these he printed one word in very big letters indeed: HONEY.

He looked at the jars and chuckled. They were labelled HONEY – but they were full of onions. Brer Bear didn't like onions – but he *loved* honey.

"There's a nice little trick going to be played on you, Brer Bear," chuckled Brer Rabbit, as he went off to fetch a sack.

He put all the jars into the sack, and then went to bed. Next morning he took the heavy sack, full of the jars, and carried it, puffing and panting, into the wood. He set the sack down near the path, half under a bush. It was the path that Brer Bear used every day!

Then he hid himself under another bush and waited for Brer Bear to come lumbering by.

Soon he heard the tattling Jack Sparrow up in the tree calling out loudly. "Here comes Brer Bear, have a care, have a care, here comes Brer Bear, beware, beware!"

Brer Bear came along, sniffing here and there as he went, his little eyes looking into every corner. He suddenly saw the sack half hidden under a bush, and went quickly over to it.

"What's this?" said Brer Bear, and he opened the sack and looked inside. At once he saw the jars, each one labelled HONEY.

"Honey! Jars of honey – big ones, too!" said Brer Bear, amazed. "I've not tasted honey for a week. Who does all this belong to?"

He called, "Anyone about?"

But nobody answered.

Brer Bear peered here and peered there, and then he picked up the sack. It was heavy but he was so strong that it felt as light as a feather to him. He put it carefully over his shoulder and set off.

"Well, if there's nobody to look after a sack of honey jars, I don't mind taking on the job myself," he said. "My, what a feast I'll have!"

Brer Rabbit watched him carrying away the sack and laughed. You wait, Brer Bear, you'll get a shock in a minute!

Brer Rabbit scampered through the wood and got right in front of Brer Bear. He ran till he came to Mr Benjamin Ram's house. Benjamin was out in his garden, smoking his pipe and digging hard.

"Mr Benjamin Ram, I've bad news for you," panted Brer Rabbit. "I put your pickled onion jars into a sack and carried it as far as the path through the wood – and I put it down for a minute under a bush – and will you believe it, someone came along and took it. It's gone."

"What? My pickled onions!" said Mr Ram, in a rage. "What next? I've paid for them, haven't I? They're mine, aren't they? How *dare* someone come along and take my sack of pickled onions. Who was it?"

"It was old Brer Bear," said Brer Rabbit, grinning. "He lives near you, doesn't he, Mr Ram? Well, you'll see him passing by in a little while and you can stop him and get them from him. I'll wait here and see fair play."

Mr Benjamin Ram was really very angry – so angry that he longed to rush at somebody and butt him hard! He waited and waited for Brer Bear to come by.

Brer Bear came in sight, the sack over his shoulder.

Mr Benjamin Ram rushed out at once, shouting, "Hey, Brer Bear, you've got my pickled onions. You drop them at once, or I'll butt you."

Brer Bear stared at Mr Ram in amazement. "*I* haven't got your onions!" he said. "I don't know what you're talking about. I've got jars of honey in here."

"I don't believe you," said Mr Ram. "Let me see, or I'll butt you."

He looked so very fierce that Brer Bear hurriedly put down the sack and undid it. Mr Ram peered inside and saw the stone jars, all labelled HONEY.

"There you are, Mr Ram," said Brer Bear. "What did I tell you? Honey!"

"Ah – that's what the *label* says!" said Brer Rabbit, sauntering up, twiddling his whiskers. "But what's *inside* the jars?"

"Honey, of course," said Brer Bear, and then he began to tell a lot of stories.

"I went to market this very morning, so I did. And I bought these eight jars of best honey. They were a fine price, too. There are no onions in these jars, it's just best honey — and what's more I'm taking it home to my old missus, this very minute."

"Well, if you bought the jars at the market full of honey, you won't mind if we look inside one, will you?" said Brer Rabbit. "Then you can laugh at us for thinking they were full of onions!" And with that he unscrewed a lid — and out came a very strong smell of pickled onions!

Brer Bear was full of astonishment. He stared at the onions as if he couldn't believe his eyes. Onions! In jars labelled HONEY. He couldn't understand it at all!

"My onions!" shouted Mr Benjamin Ram and ran straight at the surprised Brer Bear.

He butted him so hard that Brer Bear rose in the air and flew over a bush —

and landed with a thump on the other side. He got up and lumbered away as fast as he could go, very puzzled indeed.

"Well – you've got your onions," said Brer Rabbit.

"Why did you label them HONEY?" asked Mr Benjamin Ram, putting the sack over his back to take them to his house. "Seems funny to me, Brer Rabbit."

"Oh, you work it out," said Brer Rabbit, and away he skipped through the trees to catch up with poor Brer Bear.

Brer Bear was on his way home, still puzzled, rubbing a very big bruise where Mr Benjamin Ram had butted him. He wasn't at all pleased to see Brer Rabbit.

"Heyo, Brer Bear!" said Brer Rabbit. "Thanks for carrying that heavy sack to Mr Ram's for me."

"What do you mean, Brer Rabbit?" asked Brer Bear, fiercely.

"Well, it was too heavy for *me*," said Brer Rabbit. "So I left it for you to pick up. I just labelled the jars HONEY."

And with that he skipped out of Brer Bear's way, and then rolled on the ground and laughed till the tears dripped off his nose.

Poor Brer Bear – he's no match for old Brer Rabbit!

Brer Rabbit and the chimney

Now it happened once that Brer Rabbit fell fast asleep in the woods, he was so tired with chopping up logs for Christmas. There he sat, leaning against the logs, dreaming of carrot sandwiches and turnip pie.

It was bad luck that Brer Bear came along just at that very moment and saw old Brer Rabbit lying there, his mouth wide open and his eyes fast shut.

"Huh!" said Brer Bear, surprised. "Is he really asleep, I wonder? Yes, he is! Now's my chance to catch him!"

And catch him he did in his two big front paws! Brer Rabbit woke up with a mighty jump, and wasn't at all pleased to find himself being hugged by Brer Bear.

"Let me go," he said to Brer Bear. "I want to sneeze."

"Sneeze away then," said Brer Bear. "I'm not stopping you! You're coming home with me, Brer Rabbit. We'll have you for our Christmas dinner. Sneeze away!"

Brer Rabbit sneezed. "Your fur tickles my nose," he said. "Set me down. I want to sneeze again."

"Well, you sneeze then," said Brer Bear. "I told you that before. But I'm not setting you free, Brer Rabbit. You can't play tricks on me like those you play on old Brer Fox!"

And with that he hugged Brer Rabbit still closer in his arms, till Brer Rabbit had no breath left at all, and carried him all the way home with him.

When he got there he showed Brer Rabbit to Mrs Bear and the cubs. They were pleased, and sniffed him all over.

Brer Rabbit didn't like that at all.

"Shall we have him for Christmas dinner, Pa?" said one small cub.

Brer Rabbit spoke up loudly. "You won't have any Christmas dinner with your fire smoking like that," he said, nodding his head towards the fireplace. Certainly it was very smoky that morning.

"Oh, that's only the wind," said Mrs Bear. "It blows back the smoke."

"You'd better get that put right then," said Brer Rabbit, "for I'll never cook over a smoky fire! And there's another thing – you don't suppose Father Christmas will come down a sooty chimney, do you? Indeed he won't!"

"Then we shan't have anything in our stockings!" said all the cubs together.

"No. You won't," said Brer Rabbit firmly, and all the cubs began to whine and howl.

"We'll make Brer Rabbit sweep our chimney for us!" said Brer Bear, slyly. "Then Father Christmas can come down, and our Christmas rabbit will cook nicely in his pot!"

"I don't mind sweeping your chimney for you!" said Brer Rabbit. "Indeed I don't. Where is the brush and where are the poles?"

The cubs dragged them in. Brer Rabbit fixed the big round brush on to a pole and pushed it up the chimney. He screwed the second pole to the end of the first one and pushed still further up the chimney. Then he screwed on a third and a fourth.

The little cubs got very excited. "Run out and see if the brush is poking out of the top of the chimney pot yet," said Brer Rabbit, and out they all went. They came back at once.

"No. It's not out yet. Put another pole on!"

Brer Rabbit screwed on yet another pole and pushed the brush higher still. The little cubs ran out again and so did Brer Bear. But no – the brush wasn't out at the top yet!

Brer Rabbit began to puff and pant. "I'll have to have a rest, Brer Bear," he said. "All this pushing up the chimney is making my heart beat as fast as your clock."

"Sit down and have a rest then," said Brer Bear. "Don't give up just as the brush is near the top, Brer Rabbit. Sit down and take a rest."

So Brer Rabbit sat on a chair and puffed and panted for quite a long time. Then he got up and went to the chimney again. He pushed and he pushed – but the brush still didn't come out of the chimney top.

"There's something there," panted Brer Rabbit. "Maybe a brick has fallen in the top of the chimney, Brer Bear. That's why the chimney smokes, I guess, and why the brush won't come out. My word, I'll break my arms doing all this!"

He tried again – but as he was pushing hard against the side of the chimney itself, he knew quite well that the brush wouldn't come out of the top! Cunning old Brer Rabbit! He gave up again and turned to Brer Bear.

"*You* have a push," he said. "A great strong fellow like you will get the brush out of the chimney with a rush!"

Brer Bear took the pole and began to heave. "It's going up, it's going!" cried the cubs and rushed out to see if the brush was out of the top of the chimney. Brer Rabbit rushed off with them.

"It's out! The brush is out!" shouted the cubs and rushed back indoors. "How strong you are, Pa!"

Brer Bear turned round to speak to Brer Rabbit. "Well!" he said, "I did it straightaway, and . . ."

He stopped. "Hey, where *is* Brer Rabbit?"

"He came out with us to see the brush coming out of the chimney," said a small cub. "He was that excited, Pa, he danced and cheered!"

Yes – that rascal of a Brer Rabbit had danced and cheered himself right away

from old Brer Bear's house! He is safely down a rabbit-hole now, singing at the top of his voice:

"Sweep your chimney, old Brer Bear,
Sweep your chimney, I'm not there!
Hey diddle-diddle, oh what a fine joke,
Old Brer Bear is lost in the smoke!"

One of these days you'll not be able to get out of a scrape, Brer Rabbit – you'd better be careful!

Brer Rabbit and
the Bigger-Wigger

One night Brer Rabbit came to Brer Terrapin's house looking mighty scared. Brer Terrapin let him in and closed the door.

"What's sent you out into the night?" said old Brer Terrapin. "You're shaking like a leaf in the wind, Brer Rabbit. Who's after you?"

"It's Brer Wolf and Brer Fox," said Brer Rabbit. "I was a-sitting in my kitchen, eating my dinner, when I suddenly saw Brer Wolf's face looking in at my window – and when I ran into the bedroom, there was Brer Fox's face looking in there!"

"So you shot out of your house and came here," said Brer Terrapin. "Well, you've been playing such pranks on them lately, Brer Rabbit, that it's no wonder they're after you!"

"Perhaps they're on the way here to *your* house," said Brer Rabbit, after a bit. "Was that a leaf a-stirring – or was it a footfall?"

"It was the fire crackling," said Brer Terrapin. "Now you just listen to me, Brer Rabbit. I guess those two will follow you here – and I don't want a fight in *my* house, I only cleaned it up today. I've thought of a plan."

"What is it?" said Brer Rabbit. "You'll have to be quick, Brer Terrapin!"

"I'm going out," said Brer Terrapin. "And I'll scout around. If I see Brer Fox and Brer Wolf come along here, look out for some more visitors, will you?"

"What do you mean?" said Brer Rabbit, but Brer Terrapin only grinned at him.

"My door doesn't lock," he said, "so look out, Brer Rabbit. You'll have to let Brer Fox and Brer Wolf in, if they come. But be careful you don't let any other visitors in, see?"

"You're talking in riddles," said Brer Rabbit crossly – but Brer Terrapin had crawled slowly out of the house, taking his heavy shell with him.

No sooner had he gone than a bang came at the door. Brer Rabbit trembled. He didn't say a word, but got under the bed. The door swung open and in came Brer Wolf and Brer Fox.

"Nobody's at home," said Brer Fox.

"Oh, yes – somebody is," said Brer Wolf, and pointed to where one of Brer Rabbit's hind legs peeped out from under the bed. He pounced on it and dragged out Brer Rabbit, who wriggled like a snake.

"Oho! So you ran to Brer Terrapin's! We reckoned you would," said Brer Wolf. "Now – just you set a pot on the fire and heat some water. We'll have you for our supper, and maybe if Brer Terrapin comes back home we'll ask him to share it!"

"You leave me alone," said Brer Rabbit. "I've done you no harm!"

"Who hid behind the tree and called us names?" said Brer Fox.

"Who pelted us with conkers? Who poured water down our chimney?" said Brer Wolf. "Well, we've got you this time, Brer Rabbit, and we're going to keep you. Now – fill that pot."

BANG, BANG!

Everyone jumped. Brer Rabbit, too.

"Somebody at the door," said Brer Fox. "No, don't you go and open it, Brer

Rabbit. We're not letting you scamper away." He raised his voice and shouted, "Who's there?"

"I'm one of the Bigger-Wiggers," said a strange voice. "And I'm hungry. *Ooooomph, oooomph!*"

"A Bigger-Wigger! What's that?" said Brer Fox in alarm. "What a horrible voice!"

"What does a hungry Bigger-Wigger eat?" called Brer Rabbit. This must be one of the visitors that Brer Terrapin had talked about! What a joke!

"I eat foxes, bears, wolves and lions," said the voice. *"Oooomph, ooomph, ooomph!"*

"Could you eat a rabbit?" yelled Brer Fox.

"Rabbit? No! They're nothing but skin and bone," said the voice. "Give me a nice fat *wolf!*"

Brer Rabbit opened his mouth to answer, and Brer Wolf at once put his paw over it. "Don't you dare to say there's a wolf here," he muttered.

Then Brer Fox answered the voice at the door. "No. There's no wolf here. Go away, Bigger-Wigger."

"I'm hunnnnn-grrrrry!" said the voice. "We're *all* hungry. *Oooomph!*"

Brer Fox and Brer Wolf heard footsteps going away and felt most relieved. Brer Fox got up to lock the door, but there was no key.

"Suppose another Bigger-Wigger comes?" he said in alarm. "It could open the door if it wanted to. What a good thing *that* one didn't try!"

"Oh – no more Bigger-Wiggers will come," said Brer Rabbit, hiding a smile.

But just at that very moment a weird sound came to their ears. "*Plink! Plonk! Plooooonk!*"

"What's that?" cried Brer Fox, and clutched Brer Wolf so suddenly that he almost made him jump out of his skin.

"Another Bigger-Wigger!" said Brer Wolf. "And don't clutch at me like that, Brer Fox. It felt as if you were a Bigger-Wigger! Ssh!"

Another knock came at the door. BLAM! BLAM! BLAM!

"Who's there?" demanded Brer Rabbit.

"A Bigger-Wigger," said a hollow voice. "And I'm hungry. *Plink! Plonk! Ploooonk!*"

Brer Rabbit knew who *that* was! It was Mr Benjamin Ram and his fiddle. Brer Terrapin must have fetched him.

"What a horrible noise," said Brer Fox, trembling. Another knock came at the door. BLAM!

"Let me in! I'm hungry. I want a fox or a bear or a lion to eat," said the voice.

"Would a wolf do?" yelled Brer Rabbit before Brer Wolf could stop him. A pleased, gurgling noise came from outside the door, and then a fumbling as if the Bigger-Wigger was trying to find the handle.

"There's no wolf here! Go away!" yelled Brer Wolf in a panic.

"What a pity!" said the voice, and then footsteps began to walk away.

There came the sound of "*Plink! Plonk! Ploooonk!*" again, and Brer Rabbit grinned as he pictured old Mr Ram pulling at the strings of his fiddle.

"Hadn't you better get home before any more Bigger-Wiggers come?" said Brer Rabbit to Brer Wolf and Brer Fox. "They seem to be after foxes and wolves. Thank goodness they don't want rabbits."

"Maybe they don't – but *we* do," said Brer Fox, making a grab at Brer Rabbit. "Into that pot you'll go, Bigger-Wiggers or no Bigger-Wiggers!"

"Wait! Listen! *What's that?*" cried Brer Rabbit. "Look – at the window! Is it a Bigger-Wigger? Hadn't you better blow out the candle before he sees there's a fox and a wolf here?"

In a panic Brer Fox blew out the candle. Yes, there was a scuffling noise at the window. Brer Rabbit smiled to himself in the darkness – that sounded like old Brer Terrapin again. *Scuffle, scuffle, scuffle. Oooomph! Ooooooomph!*

OOOO-OOMPH! OOO-OOOMPH!
While Brer Fox and Brer Wolf clutched each other in the darkness, Brer Rabbit crept to the door. He opened it and slipped out. He shut it with a bang that made Brer Fox and Brer Wolf dive under the bed together.

"The Bigger-Wigger," they yelled. But no Bigger-Wigger came in. In fact, there wasn't another sound. They lay under the bed for a while and then came out and lit the candle, looking round fearfully.

"No Bigger-Wigger," said Brer Fox, with a huge sigh of relief.

"And no Brer Rabbit either! He's gone!" said Brer Wolf, in a rage. "Just when we had him nicely, too – and the pot's boiling ready to cook him!"

Blam-blam-blam! Brer Fox yelped in fright. Who was that at the door now? It opened – and in came old Brer Terrapin, looking just the same as ever.

"Who's this in my house?" he said to

Brer Fox and Brer Wolf. "Who comes visiting when I'm not at home? Get out, or I'll call the Bigger-Wiggers I've just seen in the wood!"

"No. Don't do that. We're going," said Brer Wolf. And they went, Brer Fox clutching at Brer Wolf in case they met a Bigger-Wigger.

Brer Terrapin laughed till his shell almost cracked. "You can come in, Brer Rabbit!" he called. "And Mr Ram, too. We'll have a nice supper together. The pot's boiling!"

In came old Brer Rabbit and Mr Benjamin Ram with his fiddle. "Thanks for your help, Mr Ram," said Brer Rabbit. "I'm glad Brer Terrapin fetched you and your fiddle – it scared Brer Fox and Brer Wolf like anything!"

There they sit in front of the fire, with a nice supper boiling in the pot. Mr Ram's got his fiddle and he's pulling at the strings. Listen! *Plink! Plonk! Ploooonk!*

Brer Rabbit buys some boots

Now one day it happened that when Brer Rabbit was at the market, he came to the old clothes stall. He had a good look round it, because he badly wanted an old coat for gardening.

There wasn't a coat that fitted him but something else caught his eye – a most *enormous* pair of boots. Brer Rabbit stared at them.

"Who used to wear those?" he asked Brer Possum, who kept the stall.

"Oh, they once belonged to Mr Lion," said Brer Possum. "But he said they hurt his feet, so he sold them to me. No good trying them on, Brer Rabbit – they're ten sizes too large for you!"

"Yes – I know that," said Brer Rabbit. "All the same, I'll have them. Here's the money. Tie them together for me and I'll carry them home round my neck."

So away he went with the enormous boots. He grinned as he went. Maybe they wouldn't fit him – but he would find them mighty useful, all the same!

Now in those days Brer Wolf was making himself a great nuisance. He was a very hungry fellow, and he was always sniffing after Brer Rabbit and Brer Coon and even Brer Terrapin. They were getting very tired of him indeed.

Brer Terrapin told Brer Rabbit to be careful at night and lock and bolt his door and windows. Brer Rabbit nodded. "I'll do that," he said. "But I'm going to scare old Brer Wolf so much that he'll soon begin locking *his* doors and windows!"

"It'll take a lot to make Brer Wolf do *that*," said Brer Terrapin. "Ah, he's a wily fellow is Brer Wolf, and a mighty strong one, too."

Now one night it began to rain, and it rained all the next day and the next one, too. Mud was everywhere and the creatures slipped and slithered about whenever they went out. Brer Rabbit had plenty of food in his cupboard so he didn't go out at all. He knew quite well that Brer Wolf was hiding in the bush round the corner. Little Jack Sparrow had sat on his window-sill and told him so!

"He's a-coming to your house tonight, Brer Rabbit," chirruped Jack Sparrow. "I sat in the bush he hid under, and I heard him tell Brer Bear so, when he came lumbering by. So you be careful, Brer Rabbit, you be mighty careful!"

Well, that night, just before it was dark, Brer Rabbit put on the great big boots he had bought at the market. My, how enormous they were on his little feet and legs! He had to tie

them on with string to keep them there.

He looked out of his window. Brer Wolf wouldn't come along till it was dark – he could safely go out now. So out he went in the enormous boots, clumping along in the mud. But what a curious thing – he walked *backwards*! Very awkward it was, too, but Brer Rabbit didn't mind. No – he walked backwards to his gate, backwards through it, and backwards in the thick mud down the road. He walked backwards into the wood just there, and then stood still and grinned.

"Now *forwards*, Brer Rabbit!" he said, and off he walked back to his house, treading carefully in the footsteps he had already made.

He went into his house and took off his boots. He locked his doors and his windows, and sat down, listening with both his ears.

Soon he heard someone coming down the muddy lane, growling all the time.

It sounded like old Brer Wolf. Brer Rabbit sat in his armchair and waited.

That was surely Brer Wolf coming through the gate! Brer Rabbit heard it creak. And now he was coming up to the front door. He had a lantern, because Brer Rabbit could see the light through the window.

"Bang-bang!" That was a *very* loud knock on the door. Brer Rabbit grinned, and called out at once.

"Who's there, disturbing me and my friend at this time of night? Go away!"

"It's Brer Wolf!" cried Brer Wolf, and banged at the door again. "Let me in. I've something to talk about with you."

"Well, I've something to talk about with my friend," said Brer Rabbit. "I'm busy. I don't want to see you."

Now Brer Wolf had already noticed the enormous footmarks down the lane, and how they went through Brer Rabbit's gate and up the path to his door. He couldn't *imagine* whose footprints they were. Surely they couldn't belong to Brer Rabbit's visitor! What an enormous fellow he must be!

"Who's this friend of yours?" he called. "He must be pretty big."

"It's Old Man Wolf-Eater," called back Brer Rabbit. "Can't you hear him rattling his teeth at the sound of your voice?"

And Brer Rabbit rattled a tin spoon inside an empty saucepan! Brer Wolf was most surprised. He looked down at the big footprints and frowned.

"I never heard of Old Man Wolf-Eater in my life," he said.

"Well, come along in and meet him then," said Brer Rabbit. "I'll open the door. But be careful of him, Brer Wolf – he's pretty hungry tonight."

Brer Wolf heard Brer Rabbit's footsteps coming to the door. "Wait!" he said. "I don't think I'll disturb you tonight after all."

"That's all right – you just come along in!" said Brer Rabbit, pretending to unlock the front door, and making a great noise about it. "Just be careful Old Man Wolf-Eater doesn't jump on you, that's all!"

Brer Wolf took one more look at the enormous footprints going up to the front door, and decided to go home at once! He didn't even stop to say goodbye!

Brer Rabbit heard him scuttling away to the front gate and grinned. "Hey, there, Old Man Wolf-Eater!" he said, as he walked back into his cosy kitchen. "Brer Wolf won't even stay to say how-do-you-do!"

But, of course, there was nobody in the kitchen, nobody at all!

"What a rude fellow Brer Wolf is, to be sure!" said Brer Rabbit, sitting down by the fire.

"And what a sly old rascal *you* are, Brer Rabbit!" he added, laughing to himself.

Brer Rabbit goes fishing

One winter's night Brer Rabbit thought he would go fishing. He went and called on Brer Terrapin to ask him if he would go too.

"I'm taking my boat," said Brer Rabbit. "I'm going to row right across the river to the other side, to a place where there's plenty of fish. You come, too, Brer Terrapin. We'll catch some good fish for breakfast this hungry weather."

"Do you mind if my old uncle comes, too?" said Brer Terrapin. "Stick your head out, Uncle, and say 'Howdy' to Brer Rabbit."

"Howdy-do!" said Brer Terrapin's old uncle, shooting his neck out suddenly

from under his big shell.

"Howdy!" said Brer Rabbit. "Yes, bring your uncle too, Brer Terrapin. Plenty of room in my boat!"

"Brrrrrr!" said Brer Terrapin as they all three went to find Brer Rabbit's boat tied up by the river. "It's freezing cold, Brer Rabbit. Good thing I've got no whiskers, or they'd freeze up like icicles! You be careful of yours!"

They all got into the boat and Brer Rabbit rowed right across to the other side of the river. "You be careful, Brer Rabbit," said Brer Terrapin, peering over the edge of the boat. "Brer Wolf lives near here, and he likes to fish about here, too. You be careful he doesn't catch you."

Just as he spoke there came a bellow from the bank. It was old Brer Wolf!

"Hey, Brer Rabbit! What are you doing in my bit of fishing-water? You get out!"

Brer Rabbit drew in his oars and threw out a small anchor.

"We'll anchor here," he said to the terrapins, not taking a bit of notice of Brer Wolf's yells. "Don't you worry about all that shouting. It's just noise and nothing else. Brer Wolf's boat has got a hole in it, so he can't come after us. We'll fish here and see what we get."

Well, they caught a whole lot of fish, and Brer Wolf got quite hoarse with shouting at them and telling them to get out of his bit of fishing-water. But pretty soon he got tired of that and went back to his home nearby.

Then Brer Rabbit suddenly noticed that he couldn't jerk his line out of the water. What was happening? He peered over the edge of the boat in the moonlight – and what a shock he got! The river was freezing fast!

"My, my!" said Brer Rabbit, startled. "We'd better get back before the river's quite frozen. It must be a bitter cold night tonight."

But the boat wouldn't move! It was stuck fast in the ice. The oars broke through the ice, but Brer Rabbit couldn't use them. He looked at the terrapins in fright.

"What'll we do? The water's frozen! We're stuck!"

"That's bad," said Brer Terrapin. "See if the ice will hold you, Brer Rabbit. Then maybe we can slide back."

Very soon the ice was hard enough to hold them. But poor Brer Rabbit couldn't go a step without falling down – and as for the terrapins, their legs just slid helplessly on the ice, and they didn't get anywhere at all!

"Brer Wolf will see what's happened when daylight comes!" said Brer Rabbit, with a groan. "He'll put on his skates and skate over the ice to the boat – and maybe he'll have rabbit-and-terrapin pie for his dinner!"

The river was frozen even harder by the morning. Brer Wolf was surprised to see it covered with ice when he peeped out of his window next morning. Aha! There was Brer Rabbit's boat stuck fast in the frozen river.

"Just wait till I get my skates on and I'll catch you all right, Brer Rabbit!" yelled Brer Wolf.

Brer Rabbit watched Brer Wolf come

down to the bank of the frozen river. He watched him put on his skates.

"If only I had some skates!" he groaned. "I'd skate out of sight in two shakes of a duck's tail! But none of us can escape because we can't even *stand* on this slippery ice!"

Then Brer Terrapin's old uncle spoke up. "Maybe I know a way to get us all free," he said. "Now see, Brer Rabbit. Put me out of the boat on to my back – and Brer Terrapin, too."

"What's the use of *that*?" said Brer Rabbit.

"Then after that you get out, too," said Brer Terrapin's uncle. "And you put one foot on my underside and the other on Brer Terrapin's – and we'll catch hold of your toes hard. And you can skate away on us, right to the other side of the river. We'll be your skates, Brer Rabbit; our shells will slide as fast as anything!"

What an idea! Brer Rabbit dropped them on to the ice, upside down, side by side. He hopped overboard himself and put a hind foot on each. The terrapins held his feet firmly in their clawed feet.

Just as Brer Wolf came skating over the ice, Brer Rabbit skated off, too, with the two upside-down terrapins for his skates! He went like the wind – and Brer Wolf was so astonished that his feet caught in one another and over he went, higgledy-piggledy, on the ice.

"Take a few lessons, Brer Wolf, take a few lessons!" yelled out Brer Rabbit, and came to a stop at the opposite bank. The terrapins let go his feet and he leapt off. He put them the right way up, and they scrambled down the nearest hole.

"Like one of my fish, Brer Wolf?" shouted Brer Rabbit, and threw one at Brer Wolf. It hit him smack on the nose – and off went wicked Brer Rabbit with his string of fish, laughing fit to kill himself. And I guess that he and the two terrapins feasted on a fine fish-pie that night!

Brer Rabbit has a laugh

Now once it happened that when carrots were scarce, Brer Wolf had plenty to sell. So everyone went to him to buy a sackful, and Brer Wolf soon began to make a lot of money.

Brer Rabbit didn't go to him till his larder was bare. Then he took a sack and a purse of money and went to Brer Wolf's with the others.

"A sack of carrots, Brer Wolf!" he said, holding out his big sack.

"I've got a sackful ready," said Brer Wolf. "Leave me your empty sack, and take this sackful."

Brer Rabbit peeped in at the top of the full sack. Big, round carrots lay there, red and well-grown.

"Thanks," he said, paid out his money, put the sack on his shoulder and went off.

But what a temper he was in that evening when he opened the sack and emptied out the carrots on the floor of his cellar!

"Only the top ones are good!" he said. "All the ones underneath are bad. I'll go and tell Brer Wolf what I think of him! I'll either have my money back or a sackful of *good* carrots!"

So off he went, and on the way he met old Brer Terrapin. "You look puffed up and fierce," said Brer Terrapin. "You going to fight someone, Brer Rabbit?"

"Yes. I'm after Brer Wolf," said Brer Rabbit. "He sold me a sack of rotten carrots."

"Ah, he had that one ready for you for a long time!" said Brer Terrapin. "Don't go near him, Brer Rabbit. He's waiting for you! You'll find yourself being cooked with some of his carrots if you go shouting outside his door."

54

Brer Rabbit marched along, fuming. But he stopped outside Brer Wolf's house, instead of marching in, to knock loudly at the door. Nobody was about but, as Brer Rabbit stood there, Mrs Wolf came out with a basket of washing. She set it down and began to hang it out on the line.

"My, my!" said Brer Rabbit. "What fine clothes Brer Wolf does have now, to be sure! He must think a mighty lot of himself!"

"They're all bought out of carrot-money," said Brer Terrapin. "They're his best clothes. He's been asked to dinner with Mr Lion, so he's told his wife to wash them and get them ready for him to wear tomorrow."

"Has he now?" said Brer Rabbit, and stared at the clothes on the line for so long that Brer Terrapin thought he must have gone to sleep on his feet!

"I've got a plan, Brer Terrapin," he said, softly. "And you're in it. Now, you just listen!"

Brer Terrapin listened, with his little head on one side. He laughed loudly. "It's a good plan," he said. "I'll help!"

Now, that night, Brer Rabbit crept into Brer Wolf's garden, where his clothes still flapped on the line, and he unpegged every single one. He pegged up instead a whole row of rotten carrots, and very peculiar they looked, dangling from the line.

Then he crept away to Brer Bear's, and pegged all Brer Wolf's grand clothes on *his* washing-line, one by one! They flapped in the moonlight, a very grand set of clothes indeed!

Brer Terrapin was with him, chuckling away. "Now it's *your* turn to help us along," said Brer Rabbit, as they went home together. "It's no good *me* doing this next bit – Brer Wolf would soon smell a rat! You know what to do and say, don't you, Brer Terrapin?"

"Ay, ay, Captain!" said Brer Terrapin. "I only hope I don't crack my shell with laughing!"

BRER
WOLF

Next morning Brer Terrapin was outside Brer Wolf's back garden, waiting. Soon he heard Mrs Wolf come hurrying out to take in the clothes she had hung out to dry the afternoon before.

She gave a loud scream and then another. "Oh! OH! Where are the clothes, the splendid, wonderful clothes? And what's this pegged up – carrots! CARROTS! Ohhhh!"

Brer Wolf came rushing out. "What's the matter? What's all this noise about? Good gracious, where are my clothes? Who's taken them – and left these carrots? It's Brer Rabbit, I know it is! I'll have his whiskers off! I'll pull his tail out. I'll . . ."

Brer Terrapin popped his head over the wall. "You sound in a grand old temper, Brer Wolf!" he said. "What's biting you?"

"Brer Rabbit's taken my new clothes!" bellowed Brer Wolf. "I guess they're hanging on his line now – or packed away in his chest. I'll pull his ears off, I'll . . ."

"Oh, your new clothes?" said Brer Terrapin, in a surprised kind of voice. "I know where *they* are!"

"You do? Well, tell me then!" said Brer Wolf, with a roar.

"Oh no. They're not at Brer Rabbit's, I'll tell you that," said Brer Terrapin. "But I'm not telling where they are — getting into trouble for nothing!"

"You just tell me!" said Brer Wolf, so angrily that Brer Terrapin put his head back into his shell.

"I'll tell you tomorrow maybe," said Brer Terrapin.

"Tomorrow! Why, I want to wear them today!" said Brer Wolf. "Don't you know I'm going to dinner with Mr Lion?"

"Much I care!" said Brer Terrapin, his head still in his shell. "Nobody's going to shout at *me*! Nobody's going to tell *me* what to do!"

Brer Wolf had to calm down. He

simply *had* to know where his new clothes were. He spoke in a quieter voice so as not to scare Brer Terrapin any more.

"You tell me," he said. "Go on, Brer Terrapin. You tell me and I'll give you a reward."

"What reward?" asked Brer Terrapin at once.

"Well – what do you want?" asked Brer Wolf.

"I'm mighty fond of carrots," said Brer Terrapin. "I'll take a sack of carrots for my reward."

"Oh no you won't," said Brer Wolf.

"Goodbye then," said Brer Terrapin, moving off slowly. "Wear your old clothes to go and see Mr Lion. What do *I* care?"

"Brer Terrapin, wait," cried Brer Wolf. "Here's a sack of carrots, see? You shall have them all if you tell me where my clothes are."

"You empty out the carrots and let me see if they're all good," said Brer

Terrapin. "I don't like the sight of those rotten ones hanging on your line, Brer Wolf. You let me see what's in the sack."

Brer Wolf emptied them out. There were six or seven bad ones and Brer Terrapin made him replace them with good ones.

"Now put the sack on my back," he said, "and I'll be off with it."

"You haven't told me where my clothes are," shouted Brer Wolf, in a panic.

"Oh no. I forgot," said Brer Terrapin. "Well, you go and look in Brer Bear's backyard, Brer Wolf, and you'll see them hanging there on his line. Aha – I reckon old Brer Bear must be going to visit Mr Lion himself, and he wants to be smart. Your clothes will just about fit him."

Brer Wolf gave such a bellow of rage that all the carrots fell off the clothes line. Then he streaked out of the garden and up the lane to the hill where Brer Bear lived with his family.

"Good day, Ma'am," said Brer

Terrapin politely to Mrs Wolf. "I'll be getting along with my sack of carrots."

And off he lumbered down the lane, the sack neatly balanced on his shelly back, humming a jolly little song as he went. He came to Brer Rabbit's house and turned in at the gate. Brer Rabbit ran out to meet him and stored the sack in his cellar at once and locked the door.

"What happened?" he asked, and laughed till the tears ran down his whiskers to hear how Brer Wolf had listened to old Brer Terrapin.

"There'll be mighty fine ructions up at Brer Bear's right now," said Brer Terrapin, cocking his head and listening. "Brer Wolf will see his clothes there, and he'll tell Brer Bear a lot of rude things – and old Brer Bear he'll come running out ready to swing Brer Wolf over the wall and into the river. My, I wish I could hear them!"

Just at that moment there came a great noise down the lane and Brer Wolf appeared, bellowing in fear, with

Brer Bear after him, smacking at him with a pair of fine red trousers, a blue coat and a yellow waistcoat!

"Take that and that!" grunted Brer Bear. "Hanging your silly clothes on my washing-line and then telling me I'd stolen them."

"Don't, don't, they'll soon be nothing but rags!" yelled Brer Wolf.

But Brer Bear didn't care if they were! The two of them disappeared down the lane, bellowing and growling and grunting, and Brer Rabbit began to laugh again.

"Old Brer Bear,
He doesn't care,
If Old Brer Wolf
Has nothing to wear!"

sang Brer Rabbit. "Come on, Brer Terrapin – let's get those carrots and make some soup. Laughing is hungry work!"

"So it is," said Brer Terrapin. "So it is!"

Brer Rabbit has some fun!

Old Brer Terrapin came down Brer Rabbit's front path as fast as he could waddle, and that was very slow indeed.

He called as he came. "Hello, Brer Rabbit, you gone to market yet? You at home?"

Brer Rabbit opened the door. He had his basket on his arm, all ready to go and do his marketing.

"What's turned you into a racehorse, old Brer Terrapin?" he said. "I've never seen you rattle along like this before."

"Listen, Brer Rabbit," said Brer Terrapin, "I was under a bush near Brer Bear's just now, and I heard him tell old Mrs Bear that he was going to lie in wait for you when you came back from market, and take your goods. He says you cheeked him yesterday, and he's going to show you what happens when people call him names."

"I only said he was an old snuffle-snout and a puffle-plonk," said Brer Rabbit.

"Whatever are they?" asked Brer Terrapin with interest. "You do think up some odd names, Brer Rabbit."

"I don't know *what* they are," said Brer Rabbit. "I just thought they suited Brer Bear when he's snuffing and puffing around. Oho – so he thinks he's going to steal my goods, does he,

when I come back from market?"

"Yes. And I've almost cracked my shell coming along here to tell you," said Brer Terrapin. "I shan't be able to walk another step today."

"You're a friend," said Brer Rabbit, "a real friend, but you'll have to do another bit of walking today all the same, Brer Terrapin. I'm going to pay old Brer Bear back for his mean little plan – and you've got to help."

"What do you want me to do?" asked Brer Terrapin, who felt that all *he* wanted to do was to sit down and put his head under his shell and go to sleep.

"Nothing much. Just be along by the old hollow tree not far from Brer Bear's house at half-past three this afternoon," said Brer Rabbit. "And carry an empty basket on your back for me. Will you do that? And I'll want you to have supper with me tonight, because there'll be chicken, and carrot soup and lettuce pie."

"Sounds good!" said Brer Terrapin.

"Right, Brer Rabbit, I'll be along by the old hollow tree. But you be careful of Brer Bear. He's in a temper, he is, and you know what kind of claws he's got!"

"Brer Bear will have to look after himself if he tries to get the better of *me*," said Brer Rabbit, "claws or no claws. Well, I'm off to market now, Brer Terrapin. See you later!"

He went off with his shopping basket, whistling like a blackbird. He shopped at the market, and bought a whole lot of things he wanted. Yes, Brer Rabbit was a good spender when he had the money!

At three o'clock he was on his way home, with a full basket, and a bag that also looked full of something. When he came to the hollow tree he gave a low whistle. Out came old Brer Terrapin, an empty basket balanced on his shell.

Brer Rabbit took the empty basket and put his full one on Brer Terrapin's back. "Can you carry that?" he said. "It's got our supper for tonight in it, and a few other things as well."

"My shell could carry a cartload," boasted Brer Terrapin. "It's as strong as iron. What am I to do now? Carry this basket home for you?"

"That's right," said Brer Rabbit. "And I'm going to walk right in front of Brer Bear's house so that he can see me and come after me."

"He's not there," said Brer Terrapin. "He's hiding in the bushes near the river."

"Better and better!" said Brer Rabbit.

He began to take some things out of the bag he carried and put them into the empty basket. They were all done up in neat little parcels.

"What are those for?" asked Brer Terrapin.

"Oh, nice little presents for Brer Bear!" said Brer Rabbit. "A packet of old nails – a piece of iron – two nice heavy stones – a big old bone – and the broken head of an axe. I picked them up from the rubbish at the market."

Brer Terrapin chuckled. "I'd rather

have you for my friend than my enemy, Brer Rabbit," he said, "and that's the truth. Well, I'll be off. It'll take me a long time to get to your house, carrying this basket."

He went off through the wood, and Brer Rabbit, carrying the other basket full of wrapped-up rubbish, went whistling by Brer Bear's house. He went towards the river, where the bridge was, keeping a sharp look-out for old Brer Bear. Ah – he must be in that bush. He was hidden except for one large foot he had forgotten about. It was sticking out of the bottom of the bush.

Just as he came up to the bush Brer Bear leapt out at him. Brer Rabbit gave a yell and dodged. He ran towards the river, and Brer Bear lumbered after him at top speed.

Brer Rabbit pretended to catch his foot on a tree-root, and almost fell. When he went on again he was limping, and groaning loudly. Brer Bear was most delighted.

69

Brer Rabbit turned and called out to Brer Bear. "Don't you chase me now, Brer Bear. You can see I'm limping. What are you chasing me for?"

"That basket of goods!" shouted Brer Bear. "And limp or no limp, I'm going to catch you and get that basket."

Brer Rabbit limped along, still groaning and with a wicked twinkle in his eye. He was almost at the river now, and Brer Bear was just behind him, puffing like a steam-engine.

Brer Rabbit turned and faced him. "You *shan't* have my goods!" he shouted, and threw his basket straight into the river nearby. *Splash*! The basket hit the water and disappeared.

Brer Bear gave a yell of dismay. He went to the bank and peered down into the river. He could quite clearly see the basket resting on the bed of the stream.

"You think you've got the best of me, Brer Rabbit, don't you?" said Brer Bear, taking off his coat. "Well, you haven't. I'm going to wade into the water and

get that basket out before everything's soaked. I'll dry the goods and keep them! That will teach you to call me names!"

"I don't need anyone to teach me to call you names," said Brer Rabbit. "I can think of plenty more myself. *You* won't be able to get that basket, old Puff-and-Blow!"

Brer Bear snorted. He took off his shoes and put his walking stick down by his coat. Then he waded into the water.

"Is it cold, Snuffly-Snout?" asked Brer Rabbit, standing on the bridge to watch.

Brer Bear snorted again. He was getting in quite deep now, and the water certainly *was* very cold.

"A bit more to the right, Puffle-Plonk," said Brer Rabbit helpfully. "Mind that hole – oooch – you're in it! Hold up, Puff-and-Blow, hold up!"

Brer Bear didn't feel the cold anymore, because he was now boiling with anger. That Brer Rabbit! That – that – oh dear, what a pity he wasn't as good as Brer Rabbit at thinking up names. He came at last to the basket, bent down too far, got the water up his nose, and spluttered.

"Now then, Splutter-Gulp!" said Brer Rabbit. "Do be careful!"

Brer Bear had got the basket at last. My, how heavy it was! Brer Rabbit had certainly been shopping that morning.

Aha – his own larder would be full in a very short while!

He took the basket to the bank. He shook himself vigorously to get the water off his thick fur. Then he sat down and began to open the parcels in the basket.

Stones! And old bones! Nails! A bit of iron! An old axe-head! Why – why – what was all this? *This* wasn't shopping goods, *this* wasn't . . .

Brer Bear got to his feet, suddenly feeling very angry. It was a trick! A mean trick! A trick to get him into the river and make him as wet as could be. Now where was that rascal of a rabbit? He would just get hold of him and shake him till his ears fell off!

But Brer Rabbit was away in the distance *hoppity-skip* – and what was more, he was wearing Brer Bear's coat, he had Brer Bear's shoes round his neck, and he was twirling Brer Bear's new walking stick as he went! Now to find Brer Terrapin!

Brer Terrapin was very pleased to see Brer Rabbit. He had just arrived at the house when Brer Rabbit himself came skipping along like a week-old lamb, twirling Brer Bear's walking stick.

"Brer Bear's soaked through," he told Brer Terrapin. "Wading in the river on a cold day like this – dear, dear, how foolish people are. Going after a lot of rubbish, too! Well, Brer Terrapin, I feel like a dinner party tonight – we'll send out a few invitations."

So they did, and everyone was most delighted to come. Even Brer Bear was asked but, of course, he didn't come. Not he! He had had enough of Brer Rabbit for one day.

"Brer Bear is the only one who hasn't turned up," said Brer Rabbit, beaming round at his guests. "I'm so sorry."

"He's in bed with a bad cold," said Brer Possum. "A very *very* bad cold, poor fellow."

"Dear me!" said Brer Rabbit. "Now – I *do* wonder how he got that?"

Brer Rabbit is so cunning!

Once, when Brer Rabbit was trotting along over a field, the wind blew some dead leaves out of the ditch into his face. Brer Rabbit got a real fright, and he tore off as if a hundred dogs were after him!

Well, it happened that Brer Fox and Brer Bear saw him running away, and they laughed to think that a few leaves had frightened Brer Rabbit. They went about among all the animals, telling them what a coward Brer Rabbit was, and how he had run away because of a few leaves.

When people met Brer Rabbit after that, they grinned slyly, and asked him whether he had had any more frights.

Brer Rabbit got very tired of it. "I'm as brave as any of you!" he said. "Yes, and braver too!"

"Well, show us what a brave man you are, then!" cried everyone, and they giggled at Brer Rabbit's angry face.

Brer Rabbit went off in a temper, and he thought and thought how he might show everyone that he was a brave fellow. Then he grinned and slapped his knee.

"I'll soon show them!" he chuckled. "My, they'll get a fright, but it will serve them right!"

Then Brer Rabbit went to work out his idea. He took seven of his tin plates, made a hole in the middle of each, and threaded them together on a thick string. My, what a noise they made when he shook the string!

Then he took a big piece of glass from his cucumber-frame and ran his wet paw up and down it to see if it would make a good noise. It did! Oh, what a squeaking, squealing noise it made!

Brer Rabbit grinned to himself.

Well, that night Brer Rabbit took the string of tin plates and the piece of glass with him and climbed up a tree not far

from Brer Fox's house. When he was comfortably settled, he began to enjoy himself.

He moaned and howled like twenty cats. He yelped like a dozen dogs. He screeched like a hundred parrots. *"Oh-ee-oo-ee, ie-oh-ee-oh, YOW, YOW, YOW!"*

Then he shook the string hard that joined the tin plates together, and they all jangled through the quiet night as if a thousand dustbins had gone mad and were dancing in a ring. *Clang, jang, clang, jang, clinky, clanky, clang, JANG!*

Brer Rabbit nearly fell out of the tree laughing at the awful noise he made. Next, he took the big piece of glass, wet his paw, and began to run it up and down the glass. *EEEEEEEE-OOOO, EEEEEEEE-OOOOO!* it went, and all the wakened animals round him shivered and shook to hear such a dreadful squealing noise.

Then Brer Rabbit jangled his plates

again. *Clang, jang, clang, jang, clinky, clanky, clang, jang!*

Brer Fox was sitting up in bed, as scared as could be. He couldn't for the life of him imagine what the noise was. It was like nothing he had ever heard before.

Brer Wolf was hiding under his bed. Brer Bear and Mrs Bear were clinging together, crying on each other's shoulders they were so frightened.

All the other animals were trembling, too, wondering what was going to happen next.

"*YOW, YOW, YOW!*" yelled Brer Rabbit. *Clinkity, clang, jang!* went his tin plates. *EeeeeeEEeeeeEEE-ooooo!* went his paw, squeaking up the glass.

At last Brer Rabbit hopped down from his tree, ran to a tumbledown shed nearby, put all his things there, and then made his way to Brer Fox's house. He knocked loudly on the door, *BLIM, BLAM!*

Brer Fox got such a shock that he fell

out of bed. "Who's there?" he said in a trembling voice.

"Me, Brer Rabbit," said Brer Rabbit. "I've come to see what all the noise is about."

"Oh Brer Rabbit, dear Brer Rabbit, I'm so glad to see you," said Brer Fox, almost falling over himself to open the door. "Do come in. I've been scared out of my life. Whatever is that noise, do you think?"

"I don't know," said Brer Rabbit untruthfully. "Unless it is old Brer Elephant rampaging around, making a frightful noise. I just came to see if you were all right, Brer Fox."

"Well, that's mighty kind of you, Brer Rabbit," said Brer Fox. "I wonder you're not afraid to be out, with all that noise around. What are you going to do now? Don't leave me!"

"I'm just off to see if Brer Wolf and Brer Bear are all right," said Brer Rabbit. "Maybe they are scared and will be glad to see me."

Off he went, and found Brer Wolf and Brer Bear just as scared as Brer Fox. My, they thought he was a very brave fellow to be out that night!

"We'll look in the morning and see if we can see any signs of Brer Elephant," said Brer Rabbit. "It's a wet and muddy night and maybe we'll find his footprints. Then we can follow them and see where he is!"

After Brer Rabbit had left his friends, he skipped and danced a bit with glee, and then he went to where he had hidden a big round log of wood, just the shape of an elephant's great foot. Brer Rabbit went all round about Brer Fox's house and Brer Bear's and Brer Wolf's, stamping the end of the big log into the mud, so that it looked for all the world as if a mighty big lot of feet had been going around there in the night.

Brer Rabbit giggled to himself when he had finished. He went back home to bed and slept well till morning.

The next day he and all the other

animals went to look for footprints. When the others saw the enormous marks in the mud they were as scared as could be.

"Those are an elephant's marks all right!" said Brer Fox. "I know an elephant's marks when I see them. My, he was around here last night all right. I wonder he didn't knock my house down!"

"Let's follow the footprints and see where they go to," said Brer Rabbit.

"I don't think I want to do that," said Brer Bear, who didn't like the look of things at all.

"What! Are you afraid?" cried Brer Rabbit. "Well, *I'm* not! I'm going to see where these footmarks lead to even if I have to go alone!"

Well, he followed the footprints in the mud, and they led him to the old tumbledown shed, as he knew they would, for he had put them there himself! Brer Fox and the others followed him at a good distance. Brer

Rabbit tiptoed to the shed and looked inside.

"Yes," said the cunning fellow, "he's in there all right! Fast asleep! I think I'll go and attack him while he's asleep!"

"What! Attack an elephant!" said Brer Wolf in the greatest astonishment. "Don't be silly."

"*I'm* not afraid of elephants!" said Brer Rabbit. "I'll go in and bang him on the head! I guess he'll rush out in a mighty hurry, so be careful he doesn't knock you all over!"

"Come back, Brer Rabbit!" called Brer Fox, as Brer Rabbit tiptoed to the shed again. "You'll only make him angry and he'll rush out and knock down all our houses!"

Brer Rabbit disappeared into the shed. He had a good laugh and then he began. He took up his string of tin plates and made them dance with a *clanky-lanky clang-jang!* He made his paw squeal up and down the glass. He yowled and howled. He took a tin trumpet from his pocket and blew hard, for he had once heard that elephants made a trumpeting sound.

Then he began to shout and yell in his own voice, "Take *that*, you great noisy creature! Take *that*, you stupid elephant! And that, and that, and that!"

Every time he said, "And *that*!" Brer Rabbit hit the side of the shed with a piece of wood and it made a terrible noise. *Crash! Crash! Crash!*

The animals waiting not far off shivered and shook. Brer Rabbit put his eye to a crack in the wall of the shed and grinned to see them.

Then he took a heap of paper bags out of his pocket, and blew them up one by one. He banged them with his hand and they went *POP!*

POP! POP! POP! POP! They sounded like guns shooting. Brer Rabbit jangled his plates again, and banged the shed with the piece of wood. You might have thought that at least twenty animals were fighting inside that shed!

And then Brer Rabbit took up the log that he had made the footprints with and sent it crashing through the other side of the shed, as if some big animal had fallen through it and was scrambling away. He began to shout.

"Run, Brer Elephant, run!" he yelled. "Run, or I'll get you! Run, run!"

Brer Fox, Brer Wolf, and all the others thought that the elephant had crashed its way out of the shed and was loose. At once they fled to Brer Fox's house and bolted themselves in, trembling. Brer Rabbit saw them from the crack in the shed and laughed fit to kill himself.

When at last he stopped laughing he made his way to Brer Fox's house, panting as if he had been having a great fight. He knocked at the door, *Blam, blam!*

"Who's there?" called Brer Fox, afraid.

"Brer Rabbit," said Brer Rabbit in a big voice. The door opened and all the animals came out. They crowded round Brer Rabbit, patted him on the back, hugged him and fussed him! My, it was grand for Brer Rabbit!

"You're a hero!" cried Brer Fox.

"The bravest creature in the world!" said Brer Bear.

"The strongest of us all!" said Brer Wolf.

"I'm glad you think so, friends," said Brer Rabbit. "There was a time when you called me a coward, and maybe if I remember which of you laughed at me then, I might treat them as I treated old Brer Elephant!"

"*We* wouldn't laugh at a brave man like Brer Rabbit!" shouted everyone at once.

"Well, just see you don't!" said Brer Rabbit, and he put his nose in the air, threw out his chest, and walked off, looking mighty biggitty! And after that the animals were very careful to be polite to Brer Rabbit for a long, long time!

Brer Rabbit's
Christmas supper

One Christmas there was very little in Brer Rabbit's larder or in Brer Terrapin's either. They sat and looked at one another gloomily. What could they have for their Christmas supper?

Now just before Christmas Brer Fox called in at Brer Rabbit's. "Heyo, Brer Rabbit!" he said. "Would you like to come and share my Christmas supper with me? You come along, do! Brer Wolf's coming and Brer Bear, too. We'd love to have your company."

Brer Rabbit felt rather doubtful. "I didn't know you'd got anything in your larder," he said.

"Aha, you wait and see!" said Brer Fox. "We'll maybe have chicken stew – ah, yes, with carrots and onions and turnips – all the things you like, Brer Rabbit."

It sounded very good. But Brer Rabbit didn't trust Brer Fox. Brer Fox was a wily one. So was Brer Rabbit. He sat and wondered if he should say yes, he'd go, or no, he wouldn't be along.

"I'll come," he said at last. "And thank you kindly, Brer Fox. I'll be along in good time for supper."

Brer Fox grinned and went. Brer Rabbit hopped along to tell Brer Terrapin. "You be careful now," said Brer Terrapin. "Brer Fox doesn't go giving food away when his larder's as empty as yours is! He'll be making a meal of *you*, Brer Rabbit, that's what he'll be doing."

"Well, he won't, Brer Terrapin, he won't," said Brer Rabbit. "You and I are going to make a nice little plan, see? And we'll have a nice little dinner all to ourselves on Christmas night. You see if we don't."

Now, on Christmas night Brer Rabbit went *lippitty-clippitty* through the woods to Brer Fox's house. When he got there he found Brer Terrapin sitting under a bush in the garden, just as he had told him to. And by him, on the ground, was a little string of bells! But Brer Terrapin wasn't ringing them yet.

Brer Rabbit hopped to the lighted window and looked in. He saw Brer Fox there, Brer Wolf and Brer Bear. On the table was a dish of raw carrots, raw turnips and onions, all waiting to be cooked in a stew. On the fire hung a big pan of boiling water. Was the chicken in there, cooking away? Brer Rabbit didn't think so, somehow!

He went to the door and knocked loudly – *blim-blam, blim-blam!* Brer Fox opened it and was full of delight to welcome Brer Rabbit.

"Well, you're nice and early!" he said. "The water's only just begun to boil – for the chicken, of course."

"Of course," agreed Brer Rabbit, sitting down.

Brer Fox sat down, too. "Well, what's the news?" said Brer Fox, throwing another log on the fire.

"Plenty of news tonight," said Brer Rabbit. "It's said that Brer Santa Claus is coming along this way with a mighty big sack of food for us all! What do you think of that?"

"There's a fine bit of news!" said Brer Bear. "I hope he'll have a pot or two of honey for me and my family."

"Sure to, Brer Bear, sure to!" said Brer Rabbit. "He's a kind and generous old fellow, Brer Santa Claus is! Oh, he'll be along soon, no doubt about it – he'll come in his sleigh with his galloping reindeer, and we'll hear his bells jingling out, so we shall!"

Just at that moment Brer Terrapin took up the string of bells he had beside him under the bush and shook them hard. The jingling came in at the window, and everyone sat up straight. *"Jingle-jingle-jingle! Jingle-jingle-jingle!"*

"There he is, for sure!" cried Brer Fox, and rushed to the door. Brer Terrapin went on ringing the bells like mad. Brer Bear and Brer Wolf ran to the door, too, and soon all three were out in the snow-covered garden.

"Sounds pretty near!" said Brer Fox, looking up into the sky, hoping to see Brer Santa Claus galloping along, ready to land on his roof. "Yes, pretty near!"

The bells certainly did sound pretty near, for they were just under the bush.

But Brer Fox didn't guess that! He and the others stood and waited for Brer Santa Claus to drop down from the sky.

Brer Terrapin crawled silently away from the bush, keeping well down under the snow. The bells sounded no more.

Brer Fox and the others felt cold and went indoors to get warm, and to see what Brer Rabbit was up to.

But Brer Rabbit wasn't there! Nor

were the carrots, the turnips or the onions! They had all disappeared with Brer Rabbit. But the pan of water was still boiling away merrily.

"Where's Brer Rabbit?" said Brer Bear. "And where's all the food?"

Brer Rabbit and the food were far away, waiting for old Brer Terrapin to come along out of the snow. And my, what a fine Christmas supper they both had, and what a fine laugh they had, too!

And when Brer Rabbit met Brer Fox the next day he shouted out to him. "Heyo, Brer Fox! Did Brer Santa Claus leave you a nice lot of presents? Sorry I couldn't wait to share them!"

Brer Fox rushed after him – but Brer Rabbit shot down a hole and laughed. Then he shook out a bit of string and jingled the bells on it.

"There's Brer Santa Claus again!" he shouted up the hole. "You go and join him, Brer Fox. That surely is Brer Santa Claus! *Jingle-jingle-jingle!*"

Brer Rabbit's Easter eggs

One day, not very far off Easter, Brer Rabbit sauntered round his garden to see how his seeds were getting on. The birds were pecking at some of them so he thought he'd put up a scarecrow.

"I'll get some hay and stuff an old sack," said Brer Rabbit to himself. And off he went to the haystack.

He had only just put his hand in to pull out some hay, when he felt something hard. "Now, what's this?" he said. "Feels like eggs to me."

He made a hole to see what it was, and, sure enough, there was a cosy little nest of chicken eggs. But goodness knows how long they had been there,

94

and Brer Rabbit knew they would be as stale as stale.

"No use," he said, sorrowfully. "No use at all. They'll be as bad as can be."

He took them out and counted them. There were six, all fine big ones, and Brer Rabbit reckoned it was a great pity that he hadn't found them before.

Then a thought came to him. He couldn't eat them himself, for he was certain they were bad – but no one else knew that, and he could give them to Brer Fox or Brer Bear, and

tell them to make an Easter pudding of them! Then, oh my! Wouldn't they pull a face when they found what the pudding tasted like!

He went indoors with them, and put them into a basket. Then he covered them neatly with a cloth, and set out to go to Brer Bear's, for he guessed Brer Fox wouldn't believe him if he said they were fresh eggs.

Brer Bear was standing at his door when Brer Rabbit arrived.

"Good day," he said. "What have you got in that basket?"

"Eggs," said Brer Rabbit. "Beautiful new-laid eggs. Brown and big – oh, fit for a king, these eggs are."

"Who are they for?" asked Brer Bear.

"They're for *you*!" said Brer Rabbit, beaming all over his face. "They're my Easter present to you. I hope you'll accept them Brer Bear, with my best wishes."

Brer Bear was so surprised he couldn't think what to say. It wasn't like

Brer Rabbit to go about giving presents, and Brer Bear wondered if there was any trick in it.

"Do you want me to give you anything for them?" he asked at last.

"*Give* me anything!" said Brer Rabbit, in a hurt sort of voice. "Of course not! Haven't I just told you these are my Easter present to you, Brer Bear? You take them and make an Easter pudding for yourself. I'm fond of you, so I've brought you my best eggs."

"Thank you, Brer Rabbit," said Brer Bear. "It's very kind of you, I'm sure."

He took the basket, and put the eggs on a dish. Then he gave the basket back to Brer Rabbit, and thanked him again.

"Don't say another word about it!" said Brer Rabbit, graciously. "I wish you a happy Easter!"

With that he ran off through the wood, chuckling to himself whenever he thought of Brer Bear using those eggs.

Now Brer Bear kept hens himself, and that evening when he went to see if there were any eggs, he found many more than usual. He brought them indoors, and put them on a dish beside those that Brer Rabbit had brought him.

"Too many eggs!" he said, looking at them. "I shall never eat them all. I'd better give some away! If Brer Rabbit's going about giving Easter presents, then I'd better, too."

So the next morning he put on his coat, and went to call on Brer Wolf.

Brer Wolf was in the garden, and Brer Bear sang out to him:

"Heyo, Brer Wolf! Here's a present for you."

Brer Wolf looked at Brer Bear, and wondered what he was up to. But Brer Bear looked so amiable and talked so kindly that soon Brer Wolf forgot to wonder about him, and took the eggs.

"They're just an Easter present," said Brer Bear. "You make an Easter pudding for yourself, Brer Wolf, and enjoy it. I've so many eggs that I'm glad to be able to give you these."

"Thank you kindly, Brer Bear," said Brer Wolf. He took the eggs out of the basket and put them in a bowl. Then he gave Brer Bear's bag back to him, and saw him out of the garden, thinking that old Brer Bear was certainly a good fellow, even if he *had* done some mighty queer things in his time.

Now that night Brer Wolf was taken ill, and when the doctor came he said that Brer Wolf had been eating too much.

"You just eat nothing but bread and water for a week," said the doctor, "or you'll certainly die. You've been greedy, Brer Wolf, that's what you've been, and you're all upset inside, worse than anyone I've ever seen."

"Oh, my!" said Brer Wolf, frightened almost out of his wits. "I promise you I'll be careful, doctor. But what am I to do with those lovely eggs over there? I've only just been given them, and surely *they* won't hurt me if I eat them?"

"They'll kill you, sure enough, Brer Wolf," said the doctor. "You give those eggs away, and don't get tempted by them, or you'll be dead this time tomorrow."

Well, Brer Wolf had only bread and water for two days, and then he got so hungry that the sight of those eggs gave him a pain.

"If I don't give them away quick as quick, I'll eat them, that's sure," he said. So he put on his hat, and took the eggs with him in a basket.

"I'll give them to Brer Fox," he decided. "He's been a good friend to me, and maybe he'll be sorry for me and give me something back for them."

Brer Fox was having a snooze on his bed, when Brer Wolf knocked on his door. He jumped up in a mighty hurry, and shouted to know who it was.

"It's Brer Wolf," said Brer Wolf. "I've brought you a present of some eggs, Brer Fox."

Brer Fox wasn't pleased to hear this, for he didn't like eggs. But he was never one to say no to a present, so Brer Wolf gave him the eggs, and told him to make himself a nice Easter pudding with them.

"Thank you, Brer Wolf," said Brer Fox, putting them into his pocket. "I hope you'll soon be able to eat a good meal."

"Oh, so do I," said Brer Wolf, and he was just going to sit down and tell Brer Fox all his troubles, when Brer Fox opened the door for him to go.

"I've got to go and see someone," said Brer Fox, who didn't want to listen to any troubles of Brer Wolf's. "You get home quickly, Brer Wolf. You look very poorly, you do – as if you were going to die, or something."

That frightened Brer Wolf, and he hurried home as fast as he could, and put himself to bed with dreadful groans.

Brer Fox took the eggs from his pocket and looked at them.

"What shall I do with them?" he wondered. "Shall I take them to Brer Rabbit's, and sell them to him cheap? I know he's fond of them."

Then a fine idea came to him. He got some red and green ink, and painted the eggs very bright colours.

"It's Easter tomorrow, and Brer Rabbit'll be wanting Easter eggs for his old woman and her children," he chuckled. "He'll buy these all right, and I'll put some money in my pocket!"

When they were dry, he went off to Brer Rabbit's. He knocked at the door, and Brer Rabbit popped his head out of the window.

"Heyo, Brer Rabbit," said Brer Fox. "Do you want any Easter eggs for your old woman? Look! I've got some fine ones!"

He took them out of his pocket, and held them up for Brer Rabbit to see.

"I don't think much of them," said Brer Rabbit. "How much are they?"

"Five pence each," said Brer Fox. "Very cheap too."

"Oh no they're not," said Brer Rabbit. "You give me them for a two pence each, and I'll buy them."

"Certainly not," said Brer Fox, and he pretended he was going off in a temper.

Well they higgled and haggled first one way and then another, and at last Brer Rabbit took the eggs, and gave Brer Fox a two pence each for them.

But Brer Fox got a fine cabbage out of Brer Rabbit as well, and he picked it himself, for Brer Rabbit wasn't going to come out and pick it, not he! He thought Brer Fox had a nasty hungry look about him.

Well, the next morning Brer Rabbit gave the eggs to his old woman, and told her to make a fine Easter pudding out of them.

When she broke them, they smelt dreadful, but she reckoned it was only the paint they were daubed with. So she served the pudding up to Brer Rabbit for his dinner, and said nothing.

Brer Rabbit took a huge spoonful and swallowed it – and then, oh, my! He sat and choked and choked and spluttered and spluttered as if he was going to die that very minute.

"These eggs are bad, as bad as any eggs could be," he shouted to his old woman. "And I'm a-going to tell Brer Fox what I think of him!"

He ran straight out, and went to Brer Fox's, coughing and choking all the way. Brer Fox was surprised to see him, and told him that Brer Wolf had given him the eggs, so he'd better go and grumble at *him*, if he wanted to make himself unpleasant.

Brer Fox had such a nasty gleam in his eye that Brer Rabbit reckoned he'd better go on to Brer Wolf's after all. But Brer Wolf, who was in bed, told him that Brer Bear had given him the eggs.

"You go along to old Brer Bear and tell him he's no friend of mine!" said Brer Wolf, when he heard how bad the eggs were. "Why, he might have poisoned me!"

So Brer Rabbit ran panting to Brer Bear's, meaning to give him such a dressing-down as he'd never had in his life before.

Brer Bear was just going to go out walking when Brer Rabbit arrived, and mighty surprised he was to find himself pummelled and punched by Brer Rabbit, in a perfect fury.

"I'll teach you to send bad eggs about!" cried Brer Rabbit. "And Brer Wolf says you might have poisoned him, so you're no friend to him, he

says! They came round to me, and my stars and moon, they were so bad they nearly killed me!"

Then all of a sudden Brer Bear sat down and began to laugh. He laughed and laughed, till Brer Rabbit had to stop punching him, and ask him what was the matter.

"Oh, you'll be the death of me, you will, Brer Rabbit!" said Brer Bear, wiping his eyes. "Why, those eggs that I gave Brer Wolf, and which came round to you, were the very ones you so kindly brought me for an Easter present! Oh, Brer Rabbit, you've been punished this time all right! If you want to kick anybody, you just go and kick yourself!"

Well, Brer Rabbit didn't wait to hear any more. He ran straight back home, and poured the pudding down the sink. Then he went to bed and thought very hard. And soon Brer Bear, Brer Wolf, and Brer Fox came under his window and laughed *very* loud indeed.

Brer Rabbit's honey

Now one day, when Brer Rabbit went to get a pot of honey out of his shed, he saw that half of it was gone.

"Look at that, now!" said Brer Rabbit, very angry. "Who's been stealing my honey pots? Yes – one, two, three, four, five, six of them. All gone. Only three left!"

Brer Rabbit stood still a minute, and then he looked in the mud outside the door. In the mud he saw the print of Brer Bear's big feet, claws and all.

"Oho, Brer Bear, so *you've* been along here after my honey, have you?" said Brer Rabbit, to himself. "Well, you think yourself mighty clever, don't you, taking honey from old Brer Rabbit. But

I'll get it back, or I'll eat my whiskers!"

So Brer Rabbit hid himself outside Brer Bear's house, waiting for old Brer Bear to go walking out, so that he might slip inside and find his pots of honey. But whenever Brer Bear stepped out, he left old Mrs Bear behind in the house – and she was every bit as big and fierce as Brer Bear himself.

"This won't do," said Brer Rabbit to himself. "If I don't get that honey soon, it'll be gone – and I'll have to eat my own whiskers."

He sat and thought. He scratched his head, and pulled at his whiskers. Then he slapped his knee, and gave a grin. It didn't take Brer Rabbit long to think of a trick – he was just full of them, any time of night or day!

Old Brer Rabbit ambled off till he came to the riverside. He whistled, and up came Uncle Mud-Turtle, a-bubbling under the water.

"Good morning to you," said Brer Rabbit. "I'd take it mighty kind of you if you'd do something for me, Uncle Mud-Turtle."

"I'll bubble-bubble-bubble do it," answered Uncle Mud-Turtle.

"Well, listen, now," said Brer Rabbit. "There's a mighty cosy hole just here, and I want you to sit in it, Uncle Mud-Turtle, and if anything comes down this hole, well, you just hold on to it for all your worth. See? You just do that, and I'll give you a taste of the finest honey you ever sipped!"

"Bubble-bubble," answered Uncle Mud-Turtle. He got himself into the cosy hole by the bank and settled down comfortably to wait. Brer Rabbit sat by the hole too, and he watched till he saw Brer Bear coming out of his house. Then Brer Rabbit began to whistle very gently, as if he was humming a tune all to himself.

Brer Bear heard him and came through the bushes. He saw Brer Rabbit with his paw just coming out of the hole, and spoke to him.

"What are you doing there, Brer Rabbit?"

"Oh, is it you, Brer Bear?" said Brer Rabbit, standing up quickly and brushing himself down. "I wasn't doing anything much."

"You just tell me what you were doing now, Brer Rabbit," said Brer Bear, moving closer.

"Well, don't you tell anyone if I tell you, Brer Bear," begged Brer Rabbit.

"You go on and tell me," said Brer Bear.

"Well, Brer Bear, it's like this," said cunning old Brer Rabbit. "Someone has been stealing my honey. It might be Brer Fox and it might be Brer Wolf. So I'm looking for a place to hide it safely. Would you think this hole a good place, Brer Bear?"

"Oh, a mighty good place," said Brer Bear at once. "Have you put any there yet, Brer Rabbit?"

"Oh, I shan't tell you *that*," said Brer Rabbit. "You won't go and tell anyone, will you, Brer Bear?"

"Not I," said Brer Bear, making up his mind to look in that hole as soon as Brer Rabbit had gone.

"Well, goodbye, Brer Bear. So nice to have seen you. *Such* a surprise!" said Brer Rabbit, and he skipped nimbly away into the bushes. He hid behind a tree and watched.

Brer Bear waited for a minute or two and then he went to the hole. He sniffed around it, and then put his big paw down to feel about for pots of honey.

And Uncle Mud-Turtle got hold of it and bit it hard! My, how he bit it! And he held on for all he was worth, biting away like a trap!

Brer Bear began to howl. He tried to get his paw out, but Uncle Mud-Turtle bit harder. Brer Bear lifted his head and yowled like fifty dogs and cats at once. Brer Rabbit slipped to Brer Bear's house and knocked on the door. Mrs Bear opened it.

"Mrs Bear, quick! Brer Bear's shouting for you!" cried Brer Rabbit.

"But he said I wasn't to leave the house," said Mrs Bear.

"Well, you listen to him," said Brer Rabbit.

So Mrs Bear listened, and when she heard the shouts and yells, the screeches and the howls, she set off down the path to the river just as fast as she could go, crying, "I'm a-coming, I'm a-coming!"

And then Brer Rabbit popped in at Brer Bear's door, saw his honey-pots on the shelf, put them into a basket, and ran out with them. On his way by the river he spied Brer Bear and Mrs Bear coming towards him. Brer Bear was nursing his right paw, and howling and crying.

"Why, Brer Bear, what's wrong?" cried Brer Rabbit, standing at a safe distance.

"What's wrong? Plenty wrong!" shouted back Brer Bear. "There's a wild animal down that hole, that's what's wrong. He's eaten your honey, sure enough!"

"Well, I've plenty here!" yelled back Brer Rabbit, and he held up his basket of pots.

Brer Bear knew the basket – and he knew the pots! He gave a yell and rushed towards Brer Rabbit. "You give me back that honey!" he shouted.

"I'll hide it down that hole!" cried Brer Rabbit, dodging away. "You go look for it there, Brer Bear!"

And the funny thing was that old Brer Rabbit *did* hide his honey down that hole – for he guessed that Brer Bear would never dare to put his paw down there again, so it would be as safe there as anywhere!

As for Uncle Mud-Turtle, he got his spoonful of honey, but he laughed so much when he took it that he choked and Brer Rabbit had to bang him on the back, and nearly broke his shell! Well, well – you never know what old Brer Rabbit will be up to next!

I'd never have guessed it, Brer Rabbit!

"**B**rer Rabbit," said Brer Terrapin, one day, hurrying in at the door. "Brer Rabbit, you'd better look out. Brer Fox and Brer Bear are after you!"

"That's nothing new!" said Brer Rabbit. "What's the matter with them now?"

"They say you charged them too much for sacks of carrots the other day," said Brer Terrapin. "They say they paid you far too much money."

"Well, they should have thought of that at the time," said Brer Rabbit. "I did charge them a good price – but after all I carried them all the way to their

homes for them."

"Yes, I know," said Brer Terrapin. "But you know what they are when they put their heads together and talk about you, Brer Rabbit. I tell you, they're coming after you and they're going to get their money back."

"Well, you sit at the front gate and just tell me when you see them coming," said Brer Rabbit. "I'm going to do a bit of cooking."

"*Cooking!* You'd better get busy and hide your money, hadn't you?" said Brer Terrapin, crawling out of the door.

"I'm just going to make a nice pie," said Brer Rabbit. "You go and keep watch for me, Brer Terrapin."

Soon Brer Rabbit was very busy. Brer Terrapin could see him through the open door. He saw him take down a pie-dish, and set out his pastry-board, and make pastry, rolling it flat. Well, well – to think Brer Rabbit could bother about cooking, when Brer Fox and Brer Bear would soon be along to search everywhere for their money!

He sat and watched the road, looking round every now and again to see what Brer Rabbit was doing. There now – he was putting the pastry on the pie-dish, and cutting it neatly round the edges, humming a little song all the time. And now he was putting the pie in the oven.

Then Brer Terrapin suddenly saw Brer Fox and Brer Bear pounding along the road at top speed. He called out at once. "Here they come, Brer Rabbit, a-panting and a-blowing, here they come!"

He crawled behind the wall, just as the two crashed in at the gateway, both as angry as could be. "Hey, Brer Rabbit, you know what *we've* come for, don't you?" growled Brer Bear, bursting in at Brer Rabbit's front door.

"To join me in a nice juicy pie?" said Brer Rabbit. "I've just this minute finished making one. It will be cooked soon – do stay and have some."

"Pies! We haven't come for PIES!" raged Brer Fox, and began to open drawers and cupboards. "*You* know what we've come for – to get back our money! You charged us double the price for those carrots, you cheat of a rabbit!"

"Well, didn't I carry them all the way home for you?" said Brer Rabbit. "Didn't I now? That made them worth double, didn't it?"

"I'm not going to argue with you, Brer Rabbit," said Brer Fox, looking under the bed. "All I want is that money! Yes, and we'll take ALL of it, not just half. That will teach you to cheat us!"

What a mess the two of them made of poor Brer Rabbit's house! They tore the blankets off the bed, they emptied pails and brushes out of the cupboard, they threw things out of every drawer – but they couldn't find any money at all, except for six pennies in an old brown teapot on the mantelpiece!

Brer Terrapin trembled at the front gate. Good gracious, what a mess Brer

Rabbit's house was in! And what would happen when Brer Fox and Brer Bear at last found the money? It was hidden *somewhere*, Brer Terrapin was quite certain of that!

Brer Fox and Brer Bear had to give up the hunt a last. They pocketed the six pennies, and that was all they found! They stamped out of the house angrily, shaking their fists at Brer Rabbit.

"All right! So the money isn't hidden in your house! We're at least sure of that! Tomorrow we'll come back and dig up the garden! And don't *you* start digging it yourself! We're going to set little Jack Sparrow to watch you, and he'll tell us just as soon as he sees you turning up any earth in your garden!"

"Oh, don't leave in such a temper," begged Brer Rabbit. "I've a pie cooking in the oven – you saw it yourself when you peeped in. Have dinner with me just to show you're friendly."

"We're NOT friendly," barked Brer Fox, and went out of the gate with Brer

Bear, slamming it so hard that it almost broke.

"Why did you ask them to stay for dinner?" said Brer Terrapin, crawling into the kitchen. "It was a silly thing to do, Brer Rabbit. They've done enough damage as it is."

"Oh, we'll soon clear that up!" said Brer Rabbit, cheerfully. "Put the cheese on the table, Brer Terrapin, and the bread, and I'll go and pick some lettuces."

Soon they were sitting having cheese and lettuce, and very nice it was, too. "What about the pie?" said Brer Terrapin. "Not that I can eat very much more!"

Brer Rabbit fetched the pie out of the oven and set it on the table. The crust was very nicely browned. Brer Rabbit took a knife and cut two pieces of crust, setting a piece on each plate. "What sort of pie is it?" asked Brer Terrapin.

"It's a *clinky-clink* pie," said Brer Rabbit, solemnly. "One of my *special* pies!" He ladled out some on a spoon, and Brer Terrapin was surprised to hear a loud clinking noise.

"Brer Rabbit! Brer RABBIT! You've cooked *money* inside this dish!" he cried. "Look at it – money! So THAT'S where you hid your money – in the pie!"

"Yes," said Brer Rabbit, eating the crust. "And don't say I wasn't hospitable to Brer Fox and Brer Bear – I asked them to stay to dinner and *share* the pie, didn't I? But they were rude and said no. Ah well – they *could* have shared the money if they'd wanted to! I'd have ladled it out on to their plates, and laughed to see their faces."

"A *clinky-clink* pie!" said Brer Terrapin, staring at the money on his plate. "Brer Rabbit, whatever will you think of next? What a hiding-place to be sure! I'd never have guessed it, never."

Nor would I, Brer Terrapin, nor would I!

You can't trick Brer Rabbit

Now once it happened that Brer Rabbit went along the lane near Brer Fox's house, and saw Brer Fox filling a sack. Brer Rabbit stopped at once.

"Heyo, Brer Fox!" he called. "What's that you're collecting? Ha! Ripe apples! Juicy windfalls! My, that tree is loaded, isn't it?"

"It is," said Brer Fox. "But not one apple do you get, Brer Rabbit! Not one. You're no friend of mine, and I'm giving you no apples!"

Brer Rabbit sat on the wall and watched, humming a jolly little tune. Brer Fox didn't like being watched. What trick was Brer Rabbit up to now?

"If you think you're going to pick up apples after I'm gone, you're wrong," he said. "I'm picking up every single one. And there's no wind, so no more will fall down. You can sit on that wall as long as you choose, you won't get a single apple."

"Who wants rotten apples?" said Brer Rabbit. "Only miserly foxes! You can keep them, Brer Fox. I like my apples off the tree, sound and ripe."

Brer Fox grinned. "Ho! Well, you're welcome to sit there and *look* at my apples," he said. "But the tree is too high for you to climb, Brer Rabbit – and you're no good at climbing, anyway. Good day to you. I'm off to make an apple pie for dinner!"

He went off with his sack. Brer Rabbit waited till he had gone into his house, and then he leapt off the wall and went round to Brer Fox's shed.

Brer Fox looked out of the window. He couldn't see Brer Rabbit on the wall, and he thought he had gone home. He grinned. Aha! That was the way to talk to that cheeky rascal!

But Brer Rabbit was very busy in the shed. He was looking for Brer Fox's ladder. Ah – there it was. He could get it out and take it to the apple tree quite easily without being seen. Brer Fox would be busy peeling his apples for a pie. He would never guess what Brer Rabbit was up to!

Brer Rabbit put the ladder over his shoulder, crept round the shed and went out the back way. He was soon in the field outside Brer Fox's garden, where the big apple tree stood.

"Up you go!" said Brer Rabbit to the ladder, and put it against the tree. "And up I go, too!"

He was soon in the tree, filling his pocket with the apples. Why should Brer Fox think that was *his* tree? It wasn't even in his garden! It belonged to anybody – and everyone should have a share of the apples.

"I'm having *my* share, anyway!" said Brer Rabbit, gleefully, as he stuffed his big pockets full. He bit into a rosy apple. It was delicious! He sat up there enjoying himself, eating three apples one after another.

Now it happened that Brer Fox wanted something out of his shed, and he went to get it. He found the door open – and the ladder gone!

"That's Brer Rabbit! He's got my ladder – and he's up that tree taking the apples – the good, ripe ones I'm saving to sell at the market!" said Brer Fox, angrily. "The rogue! The rascal! The scamp! The – the – well, I can't think of bad enough names. I'll get him! I'll teach him to take my ladder without asking, and get up that tree!"

And out of the shed went Brer Fox, grinding his big teeth, ready to eat Brer Rabbit for his dinner!

He came to the apple tree. Yes – there was his ladder. He shouted up the tree and gave Brer Rabbit such a fright that he nearly fell out.

"You up there! How dare you? I'm coming up after you, and that will be the end of you, you rascally rabbit!"

"You come on up, Brer Fox, and I'll give you one big shove, and down you'll go again!" shouted back Brer Rabbit.

Brer Fox stopped halfway up the ladder. He thought hard. Brer Rabbit *would* give him a push, there was no doubt about that – and down he would go.

Brer Fox got down the ladder again, a sudden idea making him laugh. "Stay up there all you like!" he called. "Eat apples till you look like one! I'm taking the ladder away, and I'm fetching Brer Wolf and Brer Bear. Old Brer Bear can climb up and push you down – and Brer Wolf and I will catch you. Ho, yes – we'll catch you at last. You'll taste nice with onions and carrots, Brer Rabbit, so you will!"

And with that he swung the ladder away from the tree and dropped it on the ground. Then off he went to fetch Brer Wolf and Brer Bear.

Brer Rabbit stopped eating apples. He peered down the tree. No – he really couldn't climb down it. Its trunk was too bare – he would slip and hurt himself. What was he to do then? Wait there quietly till he was caught by the others?

Brer Rabbit didn't like the look of things at all – and then he saw somebody coming by. Who was it? He peered down.

"It's Mr Benjamin Ram," he thought. "Well – maybe he'll get me out of this fix! Hey, Mr Benjamin! How do you feel today?"

"I'm suffering," said Mr Ram, looking up into the tree. "Suffering from hunger, Brer Rabbit. Not a bite have I had since yesterday. Throw me down an apple."

"One apple's no good to a hungry man!" said Brer Rabbit. "You come on up here and munch away, Mr Benjamin Ram. Why, there's a branch here so covered with apples that you could munch for a month of Sundays and you'd still find plenty!"

Mr Ram's mouth began to water. He loved apples. Good, juicy apples! But how could he get up the tree?

"I can't get up," he called. "Throw me an apple down – throw me a dozen!"

"You come on up and have a hundred or two," said Brer Rabbit, generously. "You'll find a ladder just over there, on the ground, Mr Ram. Stick it up against the tree and come and share the fruit with me. Have as much as you like! Eat all the apples on it, I don't mind!"

"That's right down generous of you, Brer Rabbit," said Mr Ram, delighted. "I'll just get the ladder."

So he got the ladder and put it against the tree. Up he went nimbly, and was soon on the branch beside Brer Rabbit. Certainly the tree was laden. Mr Ram didn't bother to fill his pockets – he just munched along a branch – munch – munch – munch. Apple after apple disappeared, and Mr Ram's beard wagged as he munched each one.

"I think I'll get down now," said Brer Rabbit, who was keeping a sharp eye out for Brer Fox and his friends. He could see them coming in the distance. "I've got enough. But you stay on up the tree, Mr Ram, and eat all you want. I'm not mean, like Brer Fox. You have all you like!"

Mr Benjamin Ram thought Brer Rabbit was the kindest fellow in the world. Munch – munch – munch. What a feast! Brer Rabbit slipped down the ladder quickly, took it away from the tree, and laid it on the ground again. Then he skipped behind a bush to see the fun, grinning all over his furry face.

Up came Brer Fox with Brer Wolf and Brer Bear. He picked up the ladder and set it against the tree. Then he called up.

"Brer Rabbit! Here comes Brer Bear. One shove from him, and you'll fall into our arms. We're waiting for you, Brer Rabbit, we're waiting!"

Mr Benjamin Ram heard all this, but as his name wasn't Brer Rabbit, he didn't answer. He went on munching. Munch – munch – munch. Brer Fox heard him and showed his teeth in a fury. "Just you wait, Brer Rabbit! Munching like that!"

Brer Bear went up the ladder. He was

very surprised to see the bearded face of
Mr Ram suddenly looking down at him.
Mr Ram didn't like Brer Bear.

"Get out," he said to him, and butted
him hard with his horns. Brer Bear
went flying out of the tree and landed
on top of Brer Fox. Brer Fox felt as if a
steam-roller had fallen on him, and he
groaned.

"Pah!" said Brer Wolf in disgust.
"Fancy you letting a little fellow like
Brer Rabbit fling you out of a tree, Brer
Bear. *I'll* go up and get him!"

And, before Brer Bear could get his
breath to warn him, up he went into
the tree. Mr Ram was waiting for him,
munching all the time. Biff! BIFF! Poor
Brer Wolf didn't even see what hit him,
and Mr Ram butted hard. He went
flying out of the tree, too, and again
poor Brer Fox was flattened out as Brer
Wolf landed heavily on top of him.

This was too much for Brer Rabbit.
He rolled on the ground beside his bush,
laughing fit to kill himself. "Ho, ho, ho!

Ha, ha, ha! Good old Mr Ram! Do it again, Benjamin, do it again. No, don't – I'll burst with laughing if you do!"

Brer Wolf, Brer Fox and Brer Bear glared at Brer Rabbit in a rage – but they couldn't chase him, they were so bumped and bruised.

"I can't run a step!" groaned Brer Fox.

But he could! Mr Ram suddenly decided that he had had enough apples, and he came down the ladder, and ran at the three of them with his horns down to butt them.

How they ran! They ran for their lives, and Mr Ram galloped after them. But he was too full of apples to catch them, and they rushed into Brer Fox's house and slammed the door in his face.

They could hear Brer Rabbit's shouts of laughter as they sank into chairs. Brer Wolf growled.

"Wait till I catch Brer Rabbit! Just wait!" he said.

Well – he's still waiting!

Roll around, Brer Rabbit

Now once Brer Rabbit learnt a new trick, and a most annoying one it was. He found out how to put his hind legs round his neck, and hold the back of his knees with his front paws. And then, having made himself into a kind of ball, he taught himself to roll along as fast as a leaf blowing in the wind!

So it happened that Brer Fox got bowled over one morning by something that hit him, *ker-blam*, on the back of his legs and laid him flat.

And then Brer Bear saw something peculiar coming towards him, rolling over and over, and he tried to get out of the way. But the strange ball hit him on his ankles and down he went!

And bless us all if it didn't happen to Brer Wolf too! Something rolled at him at top speed, tripped him up and there he was with his face in the mud, wondering what had hit him.

Now, Brer Rabbit rolled along so quickly that nobody could make out what he was, and before they could find out they were flat on the ground. Nobody *would* have found out if Brer Rabbit hadn't given himself away.

He knocked Brer Possum over, and Brer Possum fell into a holly bush and yelled the place down. Brer Rabbit almost burst himself with laughing, and he just *had* to unroll himself or he would have split his sides. He leaned against a tree and laughed.

Brer Possum heard him. He had picked himself up from the holly bush and had looked cautiously round to see what had hit him – and there, not far off, he saw Brer Rabbit holding on to a tree and laughing as loudly as a green woodpecker. And then he saw

Brer Rabbit suddenly curl himself up into a ball again, legs round his neck, and go rolling off through the wood to find someone else to bump into.

Brer Possum was very angry. He went to find Brer Bear and told him. Then they found Brer Wolf and Brer Fox and told them, too. They were all very angry with Brer Rabbit.

They tried to curl themselves up and roll too, but they couldn't. They managed to tie themselves into all kinds of knots, but somehow they couldn't manage to roll along.

"We'll have to stop this new trick of Brer Rabbit's," said Brer Fox. "It's most disrespectful of him to roll along the paths and knock us down without so much as a 'pardon me, let me pass'!"

"We'll lie in wait for him," said Brer Wolf. "You know that little glade over yonder? Well, he often comes to wash himself there, sitting in the sun and pulling first one ear down to wash and then the other. We could catch him there – and that would be the end of him!"

"Tomorrow, then," said Brer Bear, and they all agreed.

So the next day, before Brer Rabbit came along to wash his ears in the sunshine, Brer Possum, Brer Bear, Brer Fox and Brer Wolf were all in hiding behind the bushes. They waited and they waited.

Pretty soon Brer Rabbit came, rolling himself along merrily, so that it was a marvel to see him. He stood up when he came to the tree-stump, and perched himself there, humming a jolly little song.

And then Brer Bear and the others showed themselves all at once! Brer Rabbit didn't much like the look of them, but he called out, "Howdy, folks!" just as cheerfully as ever.

"You come along with us, Brer Rabbit," said Brer Wolf, with a growl.

"I'm busy," said Brer Rabbit, looking round for an escape and not seeing any.

"Busy or not, you come along with us," said Brer Fox, coming nearer.

"What's all this about?" said Brer Rabbit, pretending to be surprised.

"We're tired of that new trick of yours," said Brer Bear. "Knocking us flat like that! You ought to be ashamed of yourself, Brer Rabbit, at your age."

"I don't know my age," said Brer Rabbit, not getting off the tree-stump. "But if it's my rolling trick you're jealous of, I'd be pleased to show you how I do it."

Well, Brer Bear, Brer Possum, Brer Wolf and Brer Fox all felt they would certainly like to learn the trick. So they looked at one another, and nodded.

"Now you listen to us, Brer Rabbit," said Brer Fox. "You can show us how to do that trick, and then you're coming along with us, do you hear?"

"I hear all right," said Brer Rabbit, jumping down from the tree-stump.

"Wait," said Brer Bear hastily, afraid that Brer Rabbit would roll straight at them one after another and knock them all flat. "Wait! We're all getting behind trees to watch. So don't think you're going to do anything funny, Brer Rabbit."

"I wouldn't dream of it," said Brer Rabbit, and he rolled himself up into a ball. "Tell me when to go, and I'll roll at top speed! You're all round me, so I can't escape. You just watch and you'll see how it's done!"

"Go!" yelled all the creatures, at the tops of their voices from behind their trees.

And Brer Rabbit went. He rolled here and he rolled there, he rolled up the path and back again, and it was a wonderful sight to see him. Then he rolled right into a bramble bush, and Brer Possum squealed with laughter, because he knew how prickly a bramble bush was.

Brer Rabbit didn't come out of the bush. "He's hurt himself on the prickles," said Brer Possum, with another squeal of laughter. "He's got stuck there!"

They all went to see. But there was no Brer Rabbit in the bramble bush at all. Not a sign of him!

And then Brer Bear suddenly saw something – a big rabbit-hole in the middle of the bush! Aha! Old Brer Rabbit knew that hole well! He used it many a time when he wanted to – and he had certainly wanted to that morning!

He had just rolled right up to it – and then rolled right down it, much to the amazement of a small cousin of his who was on the way up! What a thing to do!

Brer Possum, Brer Bear, Brer Fox and Brer Wolf stood round the bramble bush and gazed angrily at the hole. "He's gone!" said Brer Bear. "We shan't see Brer Rabbit for a month of Sundays now!"

And then something hit them from behind, *ker-blam, ker-plunk*, and they all shot into the bramble bush on their faces. When they got up, there was nothing to be seen.

"If that was Brer Rabbit rolling up on us from behind again, I'll – I'll – I'll pull all his whiskers off!" spluttered Brer Bear.

It was, of course. He had rolled down the hole, out at the other end, and come back to see where the others were. One more roll and they were in the bramble bush!

There's no doing anything with old Brer Rabbit – he's worse than a bagful of monkeys!

Brer Bear's bad memory

B rer Bear always had a bad memory. He forgot things a hundred times a week, and sometimes it was very awkward.

One day he invited Brer Wolf and Brer Fox to tea the next day – but he had forgotten the invitation when the time came, and he went off to pay a call on his old aunt. So when Brer Fox and Brer Wolf turned up, expecting a most delicious tea, they found Brer Bear's house shut and nobody in at all.

They were angry with Brer Bear, and he was most upset. He sat in his front garden looking very miserable that evening when Brer Rabbit happened along.

"What's up, Brer Bear?" asked Brer Rabbit. So Brer Bear told him.

"If only I could think of something that would remind me to remember things," said Brer Bear.

"Well, why don't you tie a knot in your handkerchief every time you want to remember something?" asked Brer Rabbit. He took out his own yellow handkerchief and showed it to Brer Bear. It had a knot in it. "Look," said Brer Rabbit, pointing to the knot. "That's to remind me to buy some fresh carrots on my way home."

"What a very, very good idea!" said Brer Bear, delighted. "I'll do the same! You just come along tomorrow, Brer Rabbit, and you'll see how well I am remembering everything!"

So the next morning, Brer Rabbit ambled along, and there was Brer Bear in his house, looking at a knot in his handkerchief with a very long face.

"Brer Rabbit, this knot business is not going to work," he said dolefully. "Now

I can't remember what I put the knot there for!"

Brer Rabbit put up his hand and hid a grin. "Why, Brer Bear," he said, "*I* can tell you! You kindly asked me to dinner today!"

Brer Bear looked surprised – and well he might, for he certainly hadn't asked Brer Rabbit to dinner. But as his memory was so bad he thought Brer Rabbit might be right. He set to work to prepare a tasty dinner.

Brer Rabbit enjoyed it very much. He thanked Brer Bear and went skipping home, grinning to think how Brer Bear was so easily tricked!

The next day along went Brer Rabbit again – and once more Brer Bear was looking at his handkerchief in dismay, wondering what he had tied the knot there for.

"I simply can't remember, Brer Rabbit!" he said. "Now what *did* I tie that knot there for?"

"To remind you to give me one of your

jars of new honey!" said Brer Rabbit
at once. Brer Bear stared at him in
surprise and scratched his head. But

no amount of scratching could make him remember that he had promised Brer Rabbit some honey. Still, he liked to keep his promises, so he got down a jar and gave it to Brer Rabbit.

"All the same," said Brer Bear, "I'm *not* going to tie knots in my handkerchief any more, Brer Rabbit. It's just no use at all."

Well, Brer Bear untied the knot, and that night, although he wanted to remember quite a lot of things the next day, he didn't tie any knots in his hanky at all. He just put it on the window-sill and left it there.

Now Brer Rabbit hopped along that night and spied the handkerchief on the sill. He took it up and put two knots in it. Then he grinned and hopped off.

When he came along the next day he found poor Brer Bear in a great way, with the handkerchief on the table in front of him.

"Oh, Brer Rabbit!" said Brer Bear, "this is worse than ever! I don't even *remember* putting knots in my handkerchief – as well as not remembering what I tied them for!"

"Dear, dear!" spoke up Brer Rabbit with a grin. "It's a good thing I'm always able to help you, Brer Bear. You put *that* knot in to remind you to shake your fist at Brer Wolf when he comes by – and you put *that* one in to remind you to buy some lettuces from me this morning."

"Did I really?" said Brer Bear, astonished. "Brer Rabbit, my memory is getting worse each day!"

"Well, here are the lettuces you said you wanted," said Brer Rabbit, putting three down on the table. "Six pence, please, Brer Bear."

Brer Bear paid out six pence and looked at the lettuces in a puzzled way. He didn't like lettuces. Then why did he say he would buy some? He couldn't make it out.

"Look, here comes Brer Wolf!" said Brer Rabbit. "That's the second knot in your hanky, Brer Bear. Shake your fist at him!"

So poor Brer Bear went to the window and shook his fist at Brer Wolf when he went by. Brer Wolf was most amazed. He could hardly believe his eyes. But he was in a hurry so he didn't say anything about it.

Again that night Brer Rabbit slipped along and put a knot into Brer Bear's hanky. In the morning he arrived at Brer Bear's as usual and saw the knotted handkerchief sticking out of Brer Bear's pocket.

"Heyo, Brer Bear!" he cried. "Have you remembered what that knot is for this time?"

"Just take a look at this, Brer Rabbit," said Brer Bear, in an angry voice, and he stuck a piece of paper under Brer Rabbit's nose. On it was written in large letters:

"I HAVE NOT PUT ANY KNOTS IN MY HANKY TONIGHT.

(Signed) BRER BEAR."

"Do you see that?" said Brer Bear. "Well, I wrote that last night before I went off to sleep, Brer Rabbit. And yet there's a knot in my hanky this morning. I think perhaps *you* know something about that, don't you?"

Brer Rabbit grinned. "Well, maybe I can tell you what it's there for," he said.

"Yes – you'll tell me I asked you to tea, or something like that!" said Brer Bear. "But, Brer Rabbit, I know better this time – that knot's there to remind me to shake you till your teeth rattle in your head! Yes – that's what that knot is there for!"

But Brer Rabbit didn't wait for Brer Bear to remember any more! He scampered off, *lippitty-clippitty*, laughing to think how he had tricked poor old Brer Bear.

As for Brer Bear, he never tied another knot in his handkerchief, and he kept such a close watch for Brer Rabbit that that scamp didn't dare to go near him for weeks and weeks!

Brer Bear's party

O nce Brer Bear, Brer Wolf and Brer Fox got together and said they'd have a party, and ask Brer Rabbit too.

"You see, Brer Bear, you don't need to get any dinner ready for us if you ask old Brer Rabbit," grinned Brer Fox. "All you'll want will be three plates, three knives and forks, and one good big pot of boiling water ready on the fire!"

"All right," said Brer Bear. "I don't feel very friendly towards Brer Rabbit just now. He's always making fun of me and tricking me. I'm just about tired of him."

"Now don't you tell him that you've asked me and Brer Wolf," said Brer Fox.

"Just ask him in to dinner tomorrow, and tell him you've got something special for him. Say you've got hot chestnut-pie. He loves chestnuts."

"You leave it to me. I'll manage Brer Rabbit all right!" said Brer Bear. So he went out to find old Brer Rabbit.

He came to Brer Rabbit's house and knocked on the door, blim-blam, blim-blam!

"Who's there?" asked Brer Rabbit.

"A good friend of yours!" shouted back Brer Bear.

"Good friends ask people out to dinner!" yelled back Brer Rabbit.

"Well, that's just what I've come to ask you!" said Brer Bear. "You come along to dinner with me tomorrow, Brer Rabbit, and I'll have a nice hot chestnut-pie for you!"

Brer Rabbit was astonished to hear such a thing from Brer Bear. He poked his head out of the window and stared at him hard. Brer Bear stared back, and didn't blink an eyelid.

"All right, I'll be along," said Brer Rabbit, and popped his head in again.

Now the more Brer Rabbit thought about Brer Bear, the funnier he thought it was that Brer Bear should ask him to dinner.

"But I'll go," said Brer Rabbit to himself. "Oh yes, I'll go – and I'll come back too, though maybe Brer Bear isn't expecting me to!"

Twelve o'clock was Brer Bear's dinner-time. Brer Rabbit scuttled along to his house at half-past eleven, just to see what he could see. All he saw from outside was a mighty lot of smoke coming from Brer Bear's chimney.

"That's a mighty big fire to cook a small chestnut-pie!" said Brer Rabbit, rubbing his chin. "I'll just look in at the window and see what I can see."

So he peeped in, and all he saw was an enormous pot boiling on a big fire, and, on the table, three plates and three knives and forks. Nothing else at all.

"Funny!" said Brer Rabbit. "*Three* plates! I don't like it. No, I don't like it."

He couldn't see anyone in the room at all. Brer Wolf and Brer Fox were hidden behind a curtain, and Brer Bear was waiting by the door.

"Shall I go and knock at the door or not?" wondered Brer Rabbit. "Yes – I'll go – but Brer Bear won't get me indoors. No – I'll take him for a walk that he won't like!"

So Brer Rabbit marched round to the door and knocked loudly on it – BLAM, BLAM, BLAM!

Brer Bear opened it at once, and grinned all over his big mouth.

"Come along in," he said. "The pie is cooking."

"Well, Brer Bear, I hope you've got shrimp sauce with it," said Brer Rabbit, not going indoors. "I surely hope you have. You know, chestnut-pie is nothing without shrimp sauce."

"Well, no, I haven't got shrimp sauce," said Brer Bear. "But you come along in and taste the pie, Brer Rabbit. You won't want shrimp sauce, I know you won't."

"Oh yes, I shall," said Brer Rabbit. "And what's more, I'm not going to eat the pie without shrimp sauce, Brer Bear. If only I'd known you'd got no shrimp sauce, I'd have brought you along a whole heap of shrimps myself. There's plenty in the old well not far from here."

"I thought shrimps were only found in the sea," said Brer Bear, astonished.

"Not the sort of shrimps *I'm* talking about!" said Brer Rabbit.

"Well, never mind about shrimps," said Brer Bear, hearing an impatient noise from behind the curtains. "You come in and smell the pie, Brer Rabbit. If you don't like it, you can go."

"I tell you I'm not going to eat any pie without hot shrimp sauce," said Brer Rabbit. "I'll tell you what, Brer Bear! You get your net and come along with me to the well and fish up a few shrimps. I can't reach down, I'm too short, but you could easily reach with a net."

"Oh, all right, all right!" said Brer Bear. He went indoors and found his net.

A loud whisper came from behind the curtains: "Don't you let Brer Rabbit out of your sight, Brer Bear! Get the shrimps and bring him back at once."

"All right, all right," said Brer Bear, who was beginning to feel that he was doing all the work. He went out of the house and slammed the door. Then he and Brer Rabbit set off together.

"You see, Brer Bear, nobody who is anybody ever dreams of eating chestnut-pie without shrimp sauce," said Brer Rabbit as they went along. "I'm really surprised that you didn't think of it."

"Oh, you are, are you," said Brer Bear, feeling more and more annoyed. "Well, we'll get the silly shrimps and make them into sauce – though I guess you've got enough sauce of your own without bothering about any extra, Brer Rabbit!"

They came to the well. Brer Bear looked down into the deep, dark water. He couldn't see a single shrimp, and this was not really surprising, because there wasn't one to see!

"Ah, look! There goes a shrimp – and another – and another!" said Brer Rabbit in an excited voice. "Oooh, look at that fat fellow. Isn't he a lovely red colour!"

"I thought shrimps didn't go red till they were cooked," said Brer Bear, surprised.

"These shrimps are not like the ones you've seen before," said Brer Rabbit firmly. "Quick, Brer Bear – catch them, catch them! Put in your net!"

Brer Bear put in his net, hoping that a few shrimps would swim into it, for he couldn't see a single one to catch. But his net wouldn't quite reach.

"Lean right over, lean right over!" cried Brer Rabbit. "Then your net will reach!"

"Well, hold on to my trousers then," said Brer Bear.

So Brer Rabbit caught hold of the seat of Brer Bear's trousers, and Brer Bear leaned right over to make his net reach the water.

And then suddenly Brer Rabbit let go of Brer Bear's trousers – and down he went into the well, splish, splash!

"Oooble, oooble, ooble," gurgled poor Brer Bear, spluttering and choking as he came up again, and floundered about in the water. "Brer Rabbit, you let me go! And just look here – there isn't a single shrimp to be seen! They're not real!"

"They're just as real as your chestnut-pie, Brer Bear!" grinned Brer Rabbit, learning over the top of the well. "Yes, just as real! Goodbye! I hope you enjoy your bathe!"

He skipped off back to Brer Bear's house, dancing as he went. He poked his head in at the door and yelled to Brer Wolf and Brer Fox:

"Heyo, there! Brer Bear says there are such a lot of shrimps down that well, he wants some help. Hurry along, hurry along!"

Brer Fox and Brer Wolf rushed to the well to get some of the shrimps, but all they saw there was a very wet, very cold, and very angry bear!

"Get him out and give him some of that hot chestnut-pie!" yelled Brer Rabbit, dancing about in the distance. "He can have my share – and tell him he can have sauce from Brer Rabbit, instead of from shrimps! He'll like that, he will!"

And off went Brer Rabbit in delight, stopping every now and again to roll on the ground and laugh like twenty hyenas!

Brer Fox and Old Man Tibbar

Now once it happened that Brer Fox caught Brer Rabbit's friend, old Brer Terrapin.

Brer Terrapin was sitting snoozing in the sun, and Brer Fox tiptoed up behind him. Before Brer Terrapin could so much as open his eyes, he was tipped into a sack and taken away!

Brer Fox locked Brer Terrapin up in a dark cupboard. "I'm not going to eat you, you're too tough," he said. "But I'm going to tell Brer Rabbit I'm having you for soup tomorrow night, and, if I know old Brer Rabbit, he'll be along here to save his best friend! And I'll be having

rabbit-soup for days after that!"

Brer Fox sent a message to Brer Rabbit. "Old Brer Terrapin's in my cupboard – but tomorrow he'll be in my pot. Come and have a spoonful!"

Brer Rabbit walked up and down, up and down, when he heard that. He didn't believe that Brer Fox was going to make Brer Terrapin into soup.

"He wants me to go along and save him," said Brer Rabbit to himself. "And he thinks I'll make very nice soup myself. Oho! I know old Brer Fox better than he knows himself."

163

He sat down and wrote a note. He gave it to Brer Possum to deliver for him, and Brer Possum ran off right away.

Brer Fox took the note and read it. He read it again. Then he yelled out to Brer Terrapin in the cupboard.

"Hey, listen, old Shelly-back! Here's a note from Brer Rabbit. He's not coming to rescue you! He says he's sending Old Man Tibbar. Who's Old Man Tibbar? I've never heard of him in my life!"

Brer Terrapin sat still and thought for a minute. Then he gave a deep chuckle. "Oh, yes! I know Old Man Tibbar. You'd better be careful of him, Brer Fox. Mighty careful of him. He's a roaring, ramping terror, he is. My word, I'm glad I'm locked up in this cupboard if Old Man Tibbar's coming around. Now I wonder how Brer Rabbit got hold of *him*!"

Brer Fox stared at the note again. He didn't like the sound of Old Man Tibbar.

Well – he'd be ready for him all right! He'd lock the doors and windows, and lie low.

That night Brer Fox heard the sound of his front gate being opened. Then it was slammed. My, how it was slammed! It was slammed so hard that Brer Fox reckoned it must be off its hinges!

Then he heard a loud noise – a roaring, raging noise, a trumpeting noise, a booming noise – boom-boom-boom! Goodness gracious, could that be Old Man Tibbar's voice?

"Ah," said Brer Terrapin from the depths of the cupboard. "That sounds mighty like Old Man Tibbar. What a way he is in! Listen to him!"

Brer Fox went under the table and listened from there. He didn't like the sound of Old Man Tibbar at all. BOOM! Yowl! WHOOOOOOOOSH! And goodness gracious, hark at him stamping round the garden!

"Sounds like a whole herd of hippopotamuses!" said Brer Fox.

Thump, thump, thump, thump!

"I guess he wears outsize boots," said Brer Terrapin, who was enjoying himself.

There was no noise for a little while. Brer Fox wondered if Old Man Tibbar had gone. He crept to the window and looked out. My word – what enormous footprints showed in the beds. Old Man Tibbar must be a giant! A loud clattering noise overhead made Brer Fox pop under the table as quickly as a mouse down its hole. He sat there, shivering. Clatter, bump, clash, bang, clatter!

CRASH! Slither, clatter – THUD!

"There he goes again," said Brer Terrapin. "Jump on the roof, slither down, jump to the ground – my, what a fellow he is! It's a pity you caught me, Brer Fox. I'm bringing a whole lot of trouble on you, I am! I'm sorry for that. *I* don't want your house falling down and crashing to bits. *I* don't want a roaring, ramping fellow scrabbling for you in the ruins. *I* don't want a –"

"Be quiet," said Brer Fox, trembling so much that the table above him shook, too. "Don't keep on talking like that. If I'd known that Brer Rabbit had a friend like this Old Man Tibbar I'd never have caught you, Brer Terrapin. I'll get you out of the cupboard and you can go and call through the door to Old Man Tibbar and send him away."

"Oh, no!" said Brer Terrapin, sounding very alarmed. "I'm scared to death of Old Man Tibbar right now, Brer Fox. I'm not going to say a word to him. I'm nice and safe, I am, locked up in this cupboard. My goodness me, the roaring raging temper he's in tonight frightens me so I can hardly get my head out from my shell. He'd gobble me up as soon as look at me. He's come to get *you*, Brer Fox, not me. Brer Rabbit will come and get me when Old Man Tibbar's got *you*."

Brer Fox went to the cupboard and unlocked it. He hauled Brer Terrapin

out roughly, and pushed him across the room. He unlocked the front door in a hurry, and gave Brer Terrapin such a shove that he rolled over and over on the path outside, and lay on his back, his legs waving in the air.

"Old Man Tibbar, come and gobble up Brer Terrapin!" shouted Brer Fox, and slammed and locked the door. He stood behind it, trembling. He listened.

There wasn't a sound. Not a sound! No more trumpeting, booming and crashing. No more stamping round the house. Brer Fox wondered what was happening.

He crept to the window and looked out. Someone was bending over poor old upside-down Brer Terrapin. Someone was putting him the right way up. Somebody was laughing till his whiskers shook – and now Brer Terrapin and the somebody were walking out of the gate together.

It wasn't the great, fierce, big-booted Old Man Tibbar that Brer Fox had been so afraid of. It was somebody with long ears and long whiskers.

He carried a trumpet for trumpeting, and a drum that went boom-boom when he beat it. He wore enormous boots that Mr Lion had lent him – and all around the garden were spread bits and pieces of the broken flowerpots that he had thrown up to the roof. My word – who was he?

"It's Brer Rabbit! Brer Rabbit himself!" raged Brer Fox, and he ran to the door and opened it.

"Hey. Come back! Come back and pick up all this mess! You're a wicked storyteller, Brer Rabbit. It was you, not Old Man Tibbar – it was *you*!"

"I'm Old Man Tibbar all right!" shouted back Brer Rabbit. "Grow a few brains, Brer Fox. Spell Tibbar the other way round. Who do you get then?"

Well, well, well – to think that Brer Fox didn't guess *that*. Do tell me – did you?

Brer Fox and the little New Year

"I've had a most unlucky year," said Brer Fox to Brer Rabbit. "Everything went wrong. A chimney blew off my house, my apple tree had no apples, and my potatoes all went bad."

"It serves you right," said Brer Rabbit. "You're a mean old thing, Brer Fox. You've got plenty of good carrots, haven't you? But you don't give one away. And your turnips are bigger than you've ever had before. You'll always have bad luck if you're mean."

"If you think I'm going to give a single carrot or turnip to *you*, Brer Rabbit, you just think again!" said Brer Fox. "And don't imagine you can trick me out of anything more this year. It's almost the end of the year – two more days and the New Year will be here. I'll get good luck next year, you see if I don't."

"Well, maybe the little New Year will come by your way," said Brer Rabbit. "And if he does, you set out a little feast for him, Brer Fox. Make him think you're a fine fellow, and maybe he'll bring you good luck."

Brer Rabbit poked Brer Fox in the ribs and grinned at him in a way that Brer Fox didn't like. Off he went, skippity-skip, and left Brer Fox to think about what he had said.

Now, on New Year's Eve Brer Terrapin went a-calling on Brer Fox. He rapped at his door, blim-blam, blim-blam.

Brer Fox jumped. Surely that wasn't the little New Year coming by? He rushed to open the door.

"Oh – it's only you, Brer Terrapin," he said. "I thought maybe it was the little

New Year. Brer Rabbit had some tale about him coming by."

"He'll be along soon," said Brer Terrapin, coming in. "I'm sure I met him just now – a youngster skipping along, merry as a jay-bird. Well, Brer Fox, I've just come by to wish you a Happy New Year – and may you have more good luck than you did this last year."

"Thanks, Brer Terrapin," said Brer Fox. "Do you *really* think you met the little New Year? Maybe I'd better just set out a bit of a feast in case he comes here? He'd bring me good luck in the next twelve months then."

"That's a good idea," said Brer Terrapin.

"But *you* won't get any of the feast," said Brer Fox, sharply. "If the New Year doesn't come along *you* won't get a bite, so don't you think it! I know your little tricks."

Brer Terrapin said nothing. He just sat as if he was listening for something.

Brer Fox began to set out a nice little feast. Carrots – turnips – potatoes baked in their jackets – salted-down beans – and a loaf of crusty new bread. Brer Terrapin watched – and he listened, too, his head turned towards the door.

"I'll be going now, Brer Fox," he said, suddenly, and got up.

"Where are you going?" asked Brer Fox, at once. "What did you hear? Did you hear the little New Year? You tell him to come in here and have a bite to eat!"

"I'm not telling him *that*!" said Brer Terrapin, going out of the door. "I'm telling him to go to Brer Rabbit's, and take all his good luck with him! You don't deserve any, Brer Fox, and well you know it!"

Out he went into the night, and Brer Fox felt sure that he could hear him talking to someone. "He's telling the little New Year not to call here!" he groaned. "Well, I'll go and drag him in! When he sees this feast he'll want to stay."

So out he went, and ran down the lane to find the little New Year. But there wasn't a sign of him, not a sign. Only the cold winter wind blew and a few dry leaves rustled in the ditches.

Brer Fox shivered. He went back home, disappointed and angry. And when he got there, how he stared!

His feast had gone! Not a scrap was left of it, not a crumb! And in the middle of the table was a note, stuck against a glass:

"Thanks. Sorry you weren't at home. N. Y."

But Brer Fox knew that N. Y. didn't really stand for "New Year". *He* knew Brer Rabbit's writing when he saw it!

Then a whole lot of people arrived outside Brer Fox's house, blowing trumpets and banging drums. "New Year's in! Happy New Year, Brer Fox!"

And weren't they surprised when Brer Fox banged his door and bolted it!

"Well, well," said Brer Rabbit's voice, "anyone would think he didn't want to welcome the New Year in! Got any good luck yet, Brer Fox?"

You just wait, Brer Rabbit. You're too tricky for anything!

Brer Rabbit's great idea

Now once Brer Fox began to pay far too many visits to old Brer Rabbit, and Brer Rabbit didn't like it at all.

"I'll have to stop him somehow, Brer Terrapin," he said, when his friend came to tea with him. "One of these days he'll come visiting me when I'm having a snooze, and that won't do at all!"

"That's what he's a-planning, Brer Rabbit, that's what he's a-planning!" said Brer Terrapin. "You'd better put on your thinking-cap while you've still got a head to put it on!"

So Brer Rabbit took down his old thinking-cap and put it on. He sat down on his stool and thought very hard indeed. Brer Terrapin watched him. When he saw Brer Rabbit nod his head and smile, he knew old Brer Fox would soon be running into trouble. Brer Rabbit was planning a bit of mischief!

"You go into the woods, Brer Terrapin, and see if you can find a pair of old shoes that some Mr Man has thrown away," said Brer Rabbit. "The bigger the better. Tell me when you've found them and I'll carry them home."

It wasn't long before Brer Terrapin found an old pair of boots, in a ditch. He told Brer Rabbit.

"*Boots!*" said Brer Rabbit. "Fine, Brer Terrapin. I'll get them."

He fetched them from the ditch and took them home. He tried them on and laughed.

"I think these must belong to the Biggitty-Boggitty," he said. "Yes, I'm pretty certain they do!"

"Who's he, when he's at home?" asked Brer Terrapin, surprised.

"I don't really know, but maybe he's a cousin of Mr Lion's," said Brer Rabbit with a grin. "He's got mighty big feet, that's certain! I hope he doesn't come a-visiting me. Now, when do you think it's going to snow, Brer Terrapin? It's pretty cold today – maybe we'll get snow tonight. Then I'll be able to get busy with my great idea."

He was right. It did snow that night, and when Brer Rabbit opened his door next morning his front path was thick with dazzling white snow.

He grinned as he looked at it. Just the day for his great idea! He went indoors and put on the big old boots that Brer Terrapin had found. Then he went out on his front path, and walked slowly to his front gate. But he walked *backwards* instead of forwards! When he got to the gate he walked to his front door – but this time he walked forwards, not backwards, and carefully stepped into the big footmarks he had made all the way to the gate! So there seemed to be only one pair of footprints, and they were going up to the front door.

He put the big boots away, and then ran out to the gate, leaving his own small footmarks as usual. He went down the road, hoping he would meet Brer Fox.

"This is just about the time he comes a-calling," thought Brer Rabbit, and chuckled down in his throat. "Is that him coming along? Yes, it is."

Brer Rabbit began to walk back to his house and Brer Fox hurried to overtake him. They got to Brer Rabbit's front gate together. There, stretching up to the front door, was the row of remarkably big footmarks.

Brer Fox saw them at once and stopped. "Look, you've got a visitor, Brer Rabbit!" he said, pointing to the footmarks. "My, he must be a big fellow, just look at the size of his footprints."

Brer Rabbit stared at them as if he had never seen them before in his life. "I don't like the look of them, and that's

the truth!" he said. "Hey, look, here comes old Brer Terrapin. We'll ask him what *he* thinks about them."

Brer Terrapin came up slowly, finding it very difficult to drag his heavy shell over the snow. Brer Fox showed him the footprints up to Brer Rabbit's front door. Brer Terrapin looked at them, and then backed away, looking most alarmed.

"They look like the Biggitty-Boggitty's footmarks!" he said. "My, I don't like the look of them. I'm scurrying off home, I am!"

"The Biggitty-Boggitty – who's he?" said Brer Fox, astonished.

"I did hear say that he was a cousin of Mr Lion's," said Brer Terrapin, still looking away. "Brer Rabbit, don't you go into your house till he's gone. You can see his footprints going up to your front door – but there's none coming back. He's in there, Brer Rabbit, a-sitting by your fire and waiting for you. And that'll be the end of you,

Brer Rabbit, if you walk in at your front door!"

"I won't go in till he's gone," said Brer Rabbit. "I'm not fond of Biggitty-Boggitty. He'll go when he's tired of waiting for us. Or would *you* like to go in and have a little talk with him, Brer Fox?"

"No. Certainly not," said Brer Fox, alarmed. "I'm going to the town to do some shopping. I'll call in on my way back if the Biggitty-Boggitty's gone."

"Don't bother to do that," said Brer Rabbit. "I'll be out visiting Brer Bear. So long, Brer Fox. Keep your tail up!"

Brer Fox disappeared down the snowy road.

Brer Rabbit laughed. "Good old Brer Terrapin!" he said, and patted his friend's hard shell. "You said your little piece well. Now I'm just a-going to slip into my house, put on those big boots again, and walk to the front gate in them, so that Brer Fox will think that the old Biggitty-Boggitty has gone – and . . ."

"And what next?" asked Brer Terrapin, poking out his little head to look up at Brer Rabbit.

"Well – I rather *think* the Biggitty-Boggitty is going to visit Brer Fox's house!" said Brer Rabbit. "I wouldn't be surprised if he's going to walk all the way there and up to his front door!"

"I'll come along, too," said Brer Terrapin with a grin. So first Brer Rabbit went into his house and put on the great big boots – and then he marched in them out to his front gate and down the snowy road and all the way to Brer Fox's gate, and through it and up to his front door!

He didn't go in. He just walked back to the gate – but he walked *backwards*, putting his feet carefully into the foot marks he had already made. Brer Terrapin laughed loudly.

"It looks as if old Biggitty-Boggitty has walked up to Brer Fox's door, and gone into the house," he said. "There are no footprints coming back to the gate! Only those going to the house."

"You're right," said Brer Rabbit, pleased. "Now we'll hide behind a tree and wait for old Brer Fox to come back from his shopping!"

Brer Fox had done his shopping by now and was coming back with a fine bag of carrots and a loaf of brown bread. He stopped at Brer Rabbit's front gate to see if the Biggitty-Boggitty was still in Brer Rabbit's house. But when he saw the second row of footprints, this time coming *from* the house to the gate, he nodded his head.

"The Biggitty-Boggitty has left. He's gone somewhere else. Well, it's no good going in to visit Brer Rabbit, he said he'd be out. I'd better go home and make myself some carrot soup."

So off he went – and to his surprise he saw the enormous footprints going all the way down the road in front of him. Brer Fox felt most alarmed. He hoped that the Biggitty-Boggitty wasn't lying in wait for him.

Just before he got to his house Brer Rabbit joined him. "Hello, Brer Fox!" he said. "Done your shopping?"

"Brer Rabbit – look – there are those enormous footmarks again!" said Brer Fox. "See – they go right up to my front gate. Brer Rabbit, you don't think that awful creature has gone to my house, do you?"

"We'll soon see!" said Brer Rabbit. "Don't tremble so, Brer Fox. I won't let him hurt you. My word, yes – look there – the footprints go through your gate, and all the way up to your front door. But they don't come back!"

"He's a-sitting in there, waiting for me!" wailed Brer Fox. "Brer Rabbit, go in and see!"

"And get caught, and perhaps be eaten in one mouthful?" cried Brer Rabbit.

"I'll give you all these carrots and this loaf of bread if you'll go and fight him," said Brer Fox. "Go on, Brer Rabbit, you're not a coward, are you?"

"You give those carrots and the bread to Brer Terrapin to take to my house," said Brer Rabbit. "And then I'll go in and scare the life out of the Biggitty-Boggitty!"

So Brer Fox gave the bag of carrots and the bread to the delighted Brer Terrapin, who at once carried them off, nicely balanced on his broad shell.

Brer Rabbit rolled up his sleeves, walked boldly through the front gate and shouted loudly.

"I'm a-coming, Biggitty-Boggitty, I'm a-coming! Look out for yourself, I'm a-coming!"

He went in at the front door and banged it shut. Brer Fox stood trembling by the front gate.

And then there came such a shouting and hullaballooing from inside Brer Fox's house that it sounded as if there must be a dozen people there, all fighting one another. Brer Fox shot off behind a tree at once.

What in the wide world was going on?

There – that was a window smashing! And that sounded like a wardrobe falling down the stairs – and what on earth could *that* be? Was the Biggitty-Boggitty throwing all the pots and pans

at Brer Rabbit?

Brer Fox had never heard such a noise in his life! How thankful he was that he hadn't gone in with Brer Rabbit!

There came another crash, as the back window smashed, and at the same time a most terrible yell.

Then Brer Rabbit appeared at the front door, pulling down his sleeves. "Brer Fox – did you see the Biggitty-Boggitty running away?"

"No," said Brer Fox, in a trembling voice from behind his tree. "I guess he must have leapt out of the back window – I heard it smash. Oh, Brer Rabbit, you're a mighty fine fellow. What a fight you must have had!"

"Oh, that was nothing!" said Brer Rabbit, dusting down his clothes. "Nothing at all. And while I think of it, Brer Fox, don't come a-visiting me so often, please. I've got a bit tired of you, and I wouldn't like to lose my temper again as I had to in your house just now. I wouldn't want *you* smashing my back window and leaping through it, like an old Biggitty-Boggitty!"

"I won't come near you, Brer Rabbit," said Brer Fox, going hurriedly into his house. "I won't call on you again till you kindly ask me." Then he gave a yell. "Hey — my house is all smashed up! Who's going to pay the bill for *this*?"

"Send it to the Biggitty-Boggitty," said Brer Rabbit. "He ought to pay for that, the rascal! Good day to you, Brer Fox. I'll be away home for my carrot soup!"

And off went the rascally fellow, twirling his whiskers and singing a cheeky song.

"The Biggitty-Boggitty couldn't stay,
The Biggitty-Boggitty hurried away,
He hurried away on his great big feet,
Biggitty-Boggitty, down the street."

Put on the carrot soup, Brer Terrapin. Brer Rabbit will soon be home!